LILOU

The Misfit Daughter

The Shadyside Chronicles

ALEXANDRA PUGACHEVSKY

SASHKINA

Copyright © 2026
All rights reserved.

Printed in the United States. No part of this book may be used or reproduced in any manner whatsoever without written permission from the author. Brief passages may be quoted for the purpose of interviews, reviews, or press with permission and must be credited.
Every effort has been made to ensure this book is free from errors or omissions. This is a work of fiction. Characters, names, businesses, places, events, and incidents are either the products of the author's imagination or have been used in a fictitious manner.

ISBN: 979-8-9879977-8-9 (Paperback)
979-8-9879977-9-6 (e-Book)
Author: Alexandra Pugachevsky
Cover Design: Damonza and Diego Catto Val
Editor: Kirsten Rees | Book Editor & Author Coach

Instagram: @sashkina_author

Facebook: @sashkina.author

TikTok: @sashkina_author

Website: sashkina.com

Email: sasha@sashkina.com

Dedicated to the sacred
power that's passed from
a mother to a daughter.

Prologue

If Lilou were to believe her French mother, Katrine, France was superior to America in every way. The food, the people, the architecture, even the air – everything was better in France. As such, it led to a question that Lilou never dared to pose, even to herself: "Why hadn't her mother ever taken her to France?"

<hr>

Chapter 1
THE BEGINNING

<hr>

Katrine Kelleher moved to the United States in 1947. The gossipy neighbors called her a 'trophy wife', though never to her face. She tolerated their jealousy. It was the price a woman paid for being beautiful and classy. Katrine knew she was both. She dressed with flair, hair always done, and wore tight skirts with high heels even to go grocery shopping. She never left the house with the curlers still on, as other women did. Katrine chain-smoked, watched TV and looked visibly bored most of the day, but her house was immaculate. Dinner was ready at seven every night and was delicious.

She met Michael Kelleher at a dance in Paris two years prior, right after World War II had ended. If one were to believe Katrine's version of the story, Michael literally swept her off her feet and brought her to Pittsburgh before she understood that she had just gotten married to an American. Katrine's husband was a genial man, very ambitious, seemingly unscarred by the war. After finishing his degree with help from the GI bill, he got a job as an engineer at US Steel. Shortly after, the Kellehers bought

their house in Shadyside, an upscale Pittsburgh neighborhood. It was something Katrine insisted on:

"I grew up in Paris, in the city! I have already sacrificed
everything to move to America, so the least you can do is
get us a house in the city. Not the awful suburbs!"

In actuality, Katrine had grown up in a village outside
of Paris and had been to the City of Lights only a handful
of times, but her reputation of a city slicker had grown
into a legend and so Michael obliged.

Marianne, the couple's first daughter, was born in
1949. Katrine chose the most quintessentially French name
she could find to honor her motherland. Michael Kelleher
agreed, albeit after some hesitation. Marianne was a happy,
giggly child, and promised to grow up to be beautiful – just
like her mother.

Four years later, the Kellehers had another girl, and
this time Michael Kelleher insisted on naming the baby.
The proud father chose the most fashionable name of
1953. Linda.

"That pretty Buddy Clark song! I can't think of a
better name than Linda." He stared lovingly at the infant.
Katrine pursed her lips, but did not dare contradict her
husband. Instead of openly opposing him, she came up
with a French nickname for her second daughter and
started calling the little girl Lilou. The nickname stuck, and
that was how little Linda got to have two names. Linda was
what she was called by her father, at school, and the
outside world, and Lilou was what her mother and sister
called her. She preferred her nickname. It felt safer and
easier to pronounce, but Lilou never used it outside of the
home.

Little Linda, despite having the most popular name,
grew up shy and disengaged and had trouble fitting in. Her
playful and happy older sister loved being in the spotlight.

While Lilou tried to attract as little attention to herself as possible, feeling as if she did not belong, as if there was something wrong with her. She questioned her existence and her appearance. As long as she could remember, Lilou suffered in silence, alone and unwanted, unsure of her place in the world. She never felt close to her mother and shivered under her mother's stern stare. Marianne was kind to her, but their age difference was too much and their personalities too different for a strong bond. The only person with whom little Linda connected was her father. The only one who understood her.

Soon after Lilou turned fourteen years old, it became clear that she was not about to outgrow her mousy looks. The warm May evening started the same way as hundreds of evenings before: Lilou waiting by the front door for her father to come home from work. He entered the house exactly at six, and she rushed to him. He gave her a hug and invited her to sit next to him, so that they could read together. That hour before Katrine called the family to dinner was their ritual.

Little Linda and her father read everything together. First, board books, then pictures books, then chapter books, and then, the newspaper. That was how they had discovered Lilou's love for math. While her father read the Sports pages, she was drawn to the Business section, to the rows of stock market prices which she scrolled through in fascination. Her father explained them to her, patiently and thoroughly. Lilou sat, enthralled. An incredible world began to unfold, organized and systematic, where each number carried with it incredible potential, and everything was in its place. Lilou preferred the world of numbers to that of humans. Numbers were easy to read.

That evening, Lilou was about to read the math textbook with her father, when Katrine walked into the living room.

"What, what will become of her?!" Katrine threw her arms up to the sky in exasperation after throwing a look full of disdain at her daughter. "I can't stand it! I am trying to convince Lilou to try a new dress, and she is running away to draw formulas!" Hearing her mother's words, Lilou felt her stomach flip. She'd been sure that her mother paid her little attention and was surprised by this unprovoked attack.

"Darling, don't worry so much. Linda will figure it out. We all have our strengths," Michael Kelleher reassured his wife. "Besides, we got one smart one, one pretty one." He shifted his gaze to look at Marianne, who was twisting and turning in front of the hallway mirror, her favorite activity. Hearing her father's words, Marianne let out a giggle. She couldn't help but be happy.

"But how? I don't see how things will work out for Lilou. She only cares about math. With her looks, I mean," Katrine whispered theatrically, "she doesn't take after my side of the family at all!" She opened her eyes wide, flapped her eyelashes and pouted her lips, giving her face a doll-like appearance.

Lilou could barely hold back the tears. She knew her mother was right. Her nose was not small and adorable like her mother's, nor did she have the pretty gray eyes, nor the wavy blonde hair. She didn't inherit her mother's long legs, either. "My legs are my greatest asset," Lilou's mother would say. "American women are usually quite busty, that's their forte, but for me, it's my legs! And I make sure that men pay attention to them!"

Katrine Kelleher was one of the first women in Shadyside to wear trousers that emphasized her slender, long legs, and when she wore dresses and skirts, she would, as if by accident, use every opportunity to expose her knees.

It was Marianne who looked like their mother, long legs, wavy hair, the bright eyes. Little Linda looked a lot like her father – brown eyes, longish nose with a slight bump, and straight dirty-blonde hair. While Lilou had always known this, she'd never heard her mother openly assess her looks. Now, heard for the first time, her mother's words cut like a knife.

"Average-looking, at best, and way too bright," Katrine noted, narrowing her eyes as she examined her daughter. "What do you need all those good grades for? And in math? Science!? That's an outrage! It's not like you'll ever become an engineer, like your father." Katrine sighed and shook her head in indignation.

Michael Kelleher immediately jumped to his daughter's defense. "Katrine, you're wrong. It's great that Linda is bright. I am confident, things just have a way of working out. She'll be fine. Just wait till she turns twenty." Michael Kelleher patted Lilou on the back and gave her a reassuring look. "You go ahead, princess, read that textbook, get those straight As," he encouraged Lilou, and she obliged. Lilou climbed up the stairs, holding in the sting of tears at her mother's words, into the safety of her bedroom, which was on the top floor of their home. There, she felt protected, isolated from the entire world.

Twenty, Lilou repeated dreamily to herself, as she settled in her room and got out a textbook. She took her father's words to heart. Lilou started counting how many months she had left until her twentieth birthday. Her life was going to change after that day.

She took to translating the months into weeks, days, then hours and minutes, and then she started all over. It became an obsession, and Lilou checked the countdown to her twentieth birthday daily, first thing every morning.

———

MAY 25TH, 1968. Saturday

Lilou would never forget that day.

She had woken up and just completed the countdown to her twentieth birthday. *58 months, or 1793 days, or 43,032 hours, or 2,581,920 minutes*, Lilou repeated. She was about to calculate the seconds when she heard her mother's scream.

"Michael! Wake up! Wake up!"

Scurrying down the stairs, Lilou waited at the top of the steps, hiding behind the banister.

"What's happening?" her father asked. Lilou could hear his yawn. He usually went to bed late and rarely got up before ten in the morning on weekends.

"This! Look at this!" Katrine, her voice cracking, handed him something. Lilou could just see the corner of what appeared to be a piece of paper. Her father's trembling voice read out loud:

Maman, Daddy, and Lilou, I am moving to California with Patrick. We love each other. He doesn't want to go to Vietnam. We are going to join a commune. I'll be in touch once we settle.

"Katrine, I don't understand. Is Marianne gone?" Michael looked up at his wife. "Who is Patrick?"

"I have no idea!" Katrine yelled out. "I don't know what to do! And the graduation party is next weekend!"

Lilou's heart sank. She had seen her sister with Patrick, a football player at school. He always wore his football jacket, had ruddy cheeks, and did not seem particularly bright. *Marianne is gone!* Tears welled up in her eyes as the magnitude of it all caught up with her. *Marianne! Gone! To California.* Lilou fought back tears, crouching behind the banister. She suddenly felt lightheaded and gripped the wood tightly, so her knuckles turned white.

"Forget about the graduation party, Katrine!" Lilou heard her father's voice. "Forget everything."

The Kellehers had already planned a huge graduation party for their eldest daughter. Katrine referred to it as a 'summer festival'. The main idea behind the party, at least as far as Katrine was concerned, had been an engagement announcement, and the only hurdle was the fact that Katrine had not yet identified a suitable candidate for her daughter. It wasn't for a lack of trying.

Thanks to her mother's efforts, Marianne had met over a dozen young men, all from families with money, most of them with promising careers. The favorite among them was a lanky engineer named Ben, who had just graduated from Carnegie Mellon. Katrine invited Ben for tea and supervised Marianne's dates with the young man. Ben was yet to propose, but Katrine believed it was just a matter of time. Katrine fussed, while Marianne remained unfazed. Now the reason for Marianne's indifference towards Ben was clear: she was in love with someone else! "What am I going to tell that nice young man? This is a disgrace! Ben is clearly in love with Marianne!"

"It doesn't matter, Katrine," Michael squeezed out. By the tone of his voice, Lilou could tell that her father was furious.

"How can you say that!? Don't you care!? Marianne will ruin her reputation if anyone finds out!"

"It's already too late. And she'll come crawling back anyway, when he gets bored. When that draft dodger of hers shows his true colors. Scum like that doesn't last!" Michael Kelleher announced. Lilou heard her father's steps as he made his way back upstairs, so she scurried back to her bedroom. As Lilou closed the door behind her, she heard her mother's yelp:

"Michael! Aren't you going to go after them? Aren't you going to do anything?" But that statement was Michael Kelleher's last about his eldest daughter. It was as if she had ceased to exist.

After that day, they never spoke about Marianne. No one told Lilou what happened to her sister. She was just gone, and Lilou did not dare ask questions.

Marianne's disappearance was like a fault line that cut through the Kelleher family. Without her, they were now three separate individuals, leading three separate lives. Lilou, who had always been a solitary creature, became even more isolated. Her father, even before Marianne's disappearance keenly interested in the Vietnam war, now spent all his free time reading about Vietnam, and took it to heart each time he heard the news about the draft. Occasionally, Michael Kelleher would snigger at the 'cowards and draft dodgers', which, Lilou assumed, was in reference specifically to Marianne's boyfriend.

"All real men should fight a war at one point in their lives, like I have," Michael Kelleher would assert. "We need real men in this country! America can't lose its grip on the world. At this rate, this country will collapse, just like the Roman Empire did!"

Lilou took to obsessively reading math textbooks and continued to calculate how many minutes remained until her twentieth birthday. Now twice a day, having added a countdown before bedtime.

Katrine dealt with Marianne's disappearance another way. She discovered Mary Kay cosmetics.

Chapter 2

MARY KAY

Shortly after Marianne's disappearance, Katrine announced she was going to sell Mary Kay products and had, at last, 'found her true passion'. The very next day, she filled their home with boxes of Mary Kay merchandise. Gracefully packaged pink boxes, bottles, jars, and tubs embossed with the Mary Kay logo arrived. Katrine proudly labeled herself 'the first Mary Kay consultant in Pittsburgh.'

"I finally found my true calling!" Katrine repeated, as she lovingly unpacked the Mary Kay merchandise and arranged it in Marianne's old bedroom upstairs. "It's just temporary, but I love the natural light in her room. It will work so well as my office." Katrine rationalized her decision.

Lilou quietly observed, captivated by the flurry of activity. She had never seen her mother so busy before and wasn't sure what to make of this new development.

Several weeks later, Katrine hosted her first sales event. A group of eager women filled their living room. Lilou tiptoed out of her bedroom, hiding in her usual spot behind the banister. She listened intently, as Katrine's accented voice recounted the superior qualities of the Mary Kay cosmetics. The women cheered. Someone clapped.

"Your haircut, I love the layers! It's just like Mary Kay Ash's!" a high-pitched voice said.

"Ah bon? Thank you." Her mother purred in response in a surprising mix of French and English.

Katrine now dressed with even more care and had, indeed, recently updated her hairstyle to the layered cut that mimicked the hairdo of the brand's founder, Mary Kay Ash. Her mother's face acquired a permanent expression of arrogance mixed with obsequiousness. Very quickly, Katrine developed a following of dedicated customers who adored her. Sales grew, and so did her fame. Passersby recognized her on the street. Their telephone line was constantly busy, as Katrine received calls with referrals from friends of friends, relatives, and various acquaintances of her happy customers.

Lilou's mother loved her new status and reveled in her success. Michael Kelleher insisted it was his wife's French accent that boosted her sales, giving her an aura of superiority and secret knowledge. Katrine was sure that she was born to sell cosmetics, albeit the calling sat undiscovered until recently. Regardless of the reason, her success was undeniable.

A year later, in the summer of 1969, Katrine prepared to travel to the annual convention in Texas to celebrate her achievements with an elite circle of Mary Kay consultants from the rest of the United States. Her new suitcase lay open in Marianne's old bedroom as she packed for the trip. In the corner of the room, there was an enormous pile of documents, with receipts and pieces of paper sticking out. Each time Katrine made a sale, she stuffed a new piece of paper into the pile, forgetting about it. Before the trip, Katrine was rummaging through the papers. Suddenly, she burst into tears.

"I just can't take it anymore! This is a disaster!" She threw a look full of desperation at the mess.

"Darling, what's wrong?" Michael Kelleher rushed to the rescue. He could not stand tears and his wife rarely allowed herself to cry in his presence.

"Michael, I… I just don't understand. I can't seem to put anything together. I still haven't figured out how much I made from all of those sales. I have reports from Mary Kay, but I can't verify anything. But it's all so crazy. I get all these ribbons and stars so I know I am doing well, but I know nothing for sure!"

"But Katrine, it doesn't really matter. It's not like we need the money. It's just a hobby, right, sweetheart?" Michael gave his wife a kiss on the cheek, clearly relieved that his wife's outburst was not related to anything serious. In response, Katrine stomped her foot.

"I've found my calling, Michael! I need to know how much I am making. I need to be in control of my sales!"

"Maman, Daddy, maybe I can help!" Lilou blurted out, and before she could even understand what she was doing, walked into the room. She'd been eavesdropping on her parents' conversation, while standing outside the door on the stairwell, just as she always did. But now, a strange urge to help compelled her to intervene.

"Lilou, what are you doing here?" Katrine reached for a cigarette and gave her daughter a surprised look.

"I can add everything up and organize all your receipts, Maman." Lilou walked over to the pile of papers, throwing a surprised look at the room. The space, which had become her mother's office, felt unfamiliar and strange, as Lilou had hardly entered it since her sister left.

"All this?" Katrine pointed at the papers and sighed.

"Yes, Maman." Lilou's eyes glittered in excitement. "You know how I love dealing with numbers!"

"Yes, you've always liked math." Katrine shook her head. "I guess, why not? I've got nothing to lose!" Katrine blew a puff of smoke and sighed.

"What a great idea, Linda!" Michael Kelleher turned to his daughter and gave her a look full of pride.

"Thank you, Daddy!" Lilou smiled at her father. "So, Maman, I'd like to take a look at your receipts and invoices. Is that okay?" Lilou turned back to her mother, her voice now a near whisper, afraid that her mother would change her mind or have an outburst.

"Knock yourself out!" Katrine shrugged. "This is it." The ash from her cigarette fell on one of the documents, but she paid it no attention. With a sigh, she threw a look of disdain at her daughter and left the room without another word.

The next day, Katrine Kelleher left for Texas.

With her mother away, Lilou spent all week sorting through the documents. She stayed in Marianne's old bedroom, finding the space strangely comfortable, and went through every receipt, invoice, check, and note that her mother had accumulated over the course of the year of Mary Kay sales. Lilou loved deciphering numbers and understanding what they meant. A sale, a new customer, a new line item. She diligently reviewed every single piece of paper and assembled folders for each customer.

Despite her lack of organization, Katrine had tracked the dates of her sales diligently, so that part was relatively easy for Lilou to establish. Her mother's expenses were a bigger challenge, but Lilou accomplished the task with the help of her father, who reviewed the withdrawals from their joint bank account.

After pouring over the documents for a week, sorting through all the papers, adding and subtracting, Lilou established that her mother had made nearly ten thousand dollars in one year of Mary Kay sales. Lilou found such pleasure in going through her mother's documents, that she was sad when she finished the spreadsheet and took it to her father. The amount that her mother made was a significant contribution to the family's budget, and it made Michael Kelleher pause.

"That's quite a bit, are you sure that's right?" her father said. "Let me check, princess." Lilou's father took the spreadsheet from her hands and sat down on the sofa in the living room, his favorite spot. Lilou remained standing, fighting the urge to bite her nails. She felt a knot form in her stomach as she watched her father reading over the documentation. After several minutes, he looked up at his daughter: "You did a great job, princess! I guess we'll need to report this to the IRS." He shook his head. "Who knew your mother made so much?"

"Thank you, Daddy!" Lilou's cheeks turned red. She reveled in her father's approval. "Do you think Maman will be happy?"

"Of course, Linda, Mommy will be very happy." Her father gave her an encouraging wink.

Lilou did not share her father's confidence. Her mother was rarely satisfied. Lilou could hardly remember the last time she received any sort of praise from her mother.

Katrine was due to return from Texas the following morning, and, as Lilou drove with her father to the airport, her stomach churned at the thought of her mother's reaction. Several times during the drive, Lilou started biting her fingernails, then caught herself doing it, remembering that her mother would notice the chewed off cuticles and reprimand her.

Lilou spotted her mother among the other passengers right away. Katrine Kelleher was beaming as she walked towards them. Lilou had never seen her mother so happy and energized. Katrine embraced her husband and gave her daughter a half-smile.

"I am going to expand my business, the sky is the limit! This is what I learned at the convention," were her mother's first words, as Katrine threw a victorious look at the arrivals hall, as if expecting applause from the passengers.

"I'll even be able to sell Mary Kay products in other places in Western Pennsylvania. Just have to figure out the strategy!" The whole ride back from the airport, Lilou's mother raved about the amazing women she'd met in Texas, and gushed over Mary Kay Ash, the company founder.

"The women there were all unbelievable, so stylish, that was the real America, the crème de la crème!" Katrine exclaimed, as she took in the dreary Pittsburgh landscape. "Never in my life did I imagine that America had such amazing people! And where have they all been hiding? But it's the Southern ladies, that's where the real America is. The class! And Mary Kay herself, she's incredible. What a woman! She's a real visionary, a genius. She came up with the best idea for women like me. She really wants to help women succeed in life!" Katrine sighed and looked dreamily at a distance.

"Honey, that's great," Michael noted. The muscles of his neck tensed, as he gripped the steering wheel. Lilou sat quietly in the back, listening.

"Mary Kay Ash, is so generous and smart, and so put-together. I finally have a role model of how I'd like to be in my old age! I could make money! Real money! An income, just imagine." Katrine exclaimed.

"But I make enough, dear," Michael grunted.

"Of course, but I could get a pink Cadillac! At the convention, they awarded five of them to the best Mary Kay consultants. Can you imagine? A real Cadillac! Picture me driving one in Pittsburgh!"

"But darling, I thought it was just a hobby." Michael Kelleher responded with an ever so slight sigh, as if listening to the ravings of a friendly lunatic.

"I've always expected to work, you know. Just like my mother," Katrine said in a hushed tone and shook her head "Of course, I couldn't exactly follow in her foot-steps." From the back seat, Lilou pricked her ears up, expecting her mother to say more, but Katrine did not elaborate.

"Yes, dear," Lilou's father said, his tone now conciliatory. Lilou knew that her father did not like arguing and was powerless against his wife's arguments. Katrine Kelleher did not like to lose. As if on cue, her father put his hand on her mother's knee and squeezed it. That meant that their disagreement was over. Encouraged, Katrine continued chirping about the magical powers of Mary Kay, now discussing the superior quality of various creams and lotions.

Her father was not listening to her mother. Lilou was certain of that, though from time to time he nodded and said 'of course' and 'absolutely', thereby passively partici-pating in the one-sided conversation. When her mother fell silent for a moment, Lilou cleared her throat: "Maman, I have a surprise for you!" Lilou's face turned beet red in embarrassment.

"What is it? Are you going to prom?" Katrine turned back to face her daughter. "But it's the summer! Did a boy ask you out?"

"No, not a boy, it's something else," Lilou responded in

a near-whisper. At the mention of a boy, a knot formed in her stomach and her palms began sweating.

"Well, just tell me after I unpack." Katrine sighed and turned away.

"Yes, Maman," Lilou nodded in relief.

No one could know her secret. Lilou had to protect it at all cost from her mother's attention.

Lilou was in love with her neighbor, Gary Blacklin.

Chapter 3
GARY BLACKLIN

The first time Lilou saw Gary was July 3rd, 1968. Just a bit over a month had passed since Marianne's disappearance. The Kelleher family had settled into their uneasy routine, skirting around the issue. That morning, Lilou spent nearly twenty minutes crouching on the stairwell, hiding behind the banister and eavesdropping on her parents' bickering, desperate to hear the news about her sister. But instead, her mother and father argued about whether to attend a July 4th parade and picnic, and how to explain Marianne's absence to their friends. Her mother won, as usual, and the Kellehers would go to the annual Independence Day celebration, because, according to Katrine, it was important to 'keep up appearances'.

After work, her father was due to come home early that afternoon, so Lilou read in her bedroom, anxiously anticipating his arrival. Her mother was out, pursuing new Mary Kay clients. Lilou had gotten used to spending the long summer days bored, alone in the big house. Their home had been built in the 1880s, and was a spacious Victorian brick mansion, with generous ceilings, stained-glass windows, and ample space. She usually read in her bedroom, keeping the windows open, occasionally spying on her neighbors, which offered some entertainment and broke up the monotony of the day.

She put down the book and was about to head downstairs for a snack, when she heard the sound of a motor running. Then the bang of a car door slamming, voices. Something rolled down the street. Lilou ran to the window and peered out, pulling back the curtain, remaining concealed. Her bedroom offered a good view of the tree-lined street. Lilou saw two men hopping out of a van. One of them lit a cigarette, while the other opened the back of the vehicle.

I wonder who is moving in? Lilou thought, staring at the house across the street, which had been empty for several months. Suddenly sadness swept over Lilou, as she thought of how she could have shared this with Marianne, and how much fun they would have had speculating about the new neighbors.

"Well, that was a long drive!" Lilou heard the smoking man say.

The second one nodded, as he took out a trolley and positioned it next to the back door of the moving truck.

The movers were not very interesting, and Lilou decided to grab her snack downstairs. She was about to head to the kitchen, when a black sedan pulled up to the curb, parking right behind the van. Lilou froze in place. A young man emerged from the car.

She slowly took in his broad shoulders, the impressive stature. He said something to the movers, and they immediately started to unload the van. The young man looked so strong, and yet somehow vulnerable, as he brushed the bangs off his forehead and squinted at the sun.

Her heart stopped. She thought he'd noticed her as he

looked up. Lilou stepped back, and when she looked again, the young man had stacked several boxes on top of each other and was deftly carrying them into the house. She noticed his bulging muscles.

Our new neighbor! Lilou breathed out. *I wonder what his name is.* She forgot all about the book she'd been reading, her father, the snack. Nothing else mattered. Lilou froze by the window, waiting for the young man to come back outside and get more boxes. He reappeared, exchanging a few words with the movers. Just then, her father pulled up in his Ford. Lilou observed, as Michael Kelleher walked over to the young man.

"You must be our new neighbor." Lilou's father extended his hand.

"Gary Blacklin," the young man answered in a low voice. He looked confident as he shook her father's hand. Lilou's heart pounded so hard, she felt as if she would suffocate. *Gary,* Lilou repeated, rolling the R gently between her lips. *Gary and Linda.*

Lilou had never believed in love at first sight. But now she knew it was real. *This is what they mean. This is love,* she thought, staring down at the new neighbor.

"We live right next door," she heard her father say. "Where did you folks move from?"

"From Indiana. My parents should be arriving in a few." Lilou heard the young man respond.

His voice is so melodic! she thought. *I could go outside and say hello myself.* Although the idea crossed her mind, almost immediately she felt her palms sweating, fear gripping her tightly. She stepped back from the curtain. *No, not yet, not yet,* she told herself, as she sat down on the bed to catch her breath.

To calm her nerves, Lilou checked how much time remained until her twentieth birthday. She'd done the countdown that morning, but was compelled to do so again. *1754 days until I am twenty. Not that long.* A victorious smile appeared on her face, and Lilou headed downstairs to greet her father.

"Hi, Daddy!" she said. Lilou had calculated the moment just right, and was by the door the moment her father walked into the house.

"Hello, princess. I just met our new neighbor." Her father smiled at her.

"What neighbor?" Lilou feigned ignorance.

"A family from Indiana is moving across the street A nice young man was unpacking the van. Seems to be just the right age for the draft."

"The draft?" Lilou could barely hold back her astonishment. The handsome neighbor could not possibly go to war.

"Yes, Linda, we are at war for freedom." Michael Kelleher cleared his throat. Lilou could tell that her father was about to give a speech about Vietnam and the importance of serving in the military, but at that moment, her mother returned home, putting an end to their conversation.

"I just saw the movers for the house next door," Katrine noted. "Wouldn't it be great if the mother of the family became a client of mine?"

"Yes, dear," Lilou's father nodded in agreement.

In the following few days, Lilou dedicated herself to learning as much as possible about the new neighbor, spending even more time in her bedroom. She kept her window open, lying in wait for Gary. To her dismay, he rarely appeared outside, and when he did, it was to get into the car and drive off. She saw his parents once. They looked ordinary, an average-looking man and a slightly plump woman, both likely in their forties. Lilou could not understand how two completely regular people could have produced such an incredible offspring. She dreamed about meeting Gary in person, though her stomach flipped every time she thought of seeing him, and so she stopped herself. Instead, she counted down to the day she would turn twenty. *Everything will happen then.* The thought calmed her.

A week after the Blacklins had moved in, Lilou was walking back from Kroger's. A day prior, Katrine had accidentally confused margarine with butter at the grocery store. She discovered her mistake while in the middle of making dinner and went into a near meltdown.

"This is an outrage! I cannot cook with margarine! They do this on purpose. The packaging is the same!"

"Maman, it says margarine right here." Lilou pointed to the package.

Katrine rolled her eyes. "You are not being helpful! Please run to the store and get us some butter!" Her mother ordered in a tone that was bordering on hysterical. She reached for a cigarette and exhaled.

"Of course, Maman!" Lilou nodded and rushed to Kroger's. Twenty minutes later, on her way back home, she was out of breath as the afternoon heat beat down on her. In front of the Blacklin residence, Lilou slowed down. She badly wanted to catch sight of her new neighbor, and this was the perfect opportunity. *Maman can wait an extra minute,* Lilou thought.

Stopping right next to the Blacklins' front door, she stood still in the shade of a tall oak tree. Lilou dropped the bag with the butter on the ground and fanned herself. She'd seen her mother do this hundreds of times, a gesture both elegant and demure, and for a moment she pictured herself as a damsel about to meet a handsome gentleman at a ball.

"Hot day!"

Lilou recognized the voice right away. It was him. Everything stopped. Her heart started racing, and she felt her cheeks flush. Lilou slowly turned around and was now face-to-face with Gary. *Am I dreaming?* The thought flashed through her mind. Up close, Gary was even more attractive than she had imagined.

"Hey, I'm Gary. Gary Blacklin. We moved in last week." The young man smiled and extended his hand. By now, she knew her cheeks were beet-red.

"Hi," Lilou croaked.

"So, what's your name?" Gary kept smiling and tilted his head slightly. He looked like a curious bird, and Lilou found the expression on his face adorable.

"Lilou," she said in a near whisper. "Linda. My name is Linda." Lilou corrected herself.

"You got two names?" Gary ran his hand through his hair.

"Kind of. One is a nickname."

"That's groovy." He gave her an encouraging smile.

Her heart melted. "We live right here!" Lilou pointed to her house.

"I think I met your father the other day."

"Oh, really?" Lilou responded. Her heart leaped. She felt magic in the air. *He knows who I am! He likes me!*

"Yeah. So how old are you, Linda?"

"I am fifteen." Lilou responded.

"You must be a sophomore, then, am I right?" She nodded. "I'll be a senior this year. Will be enrolling at Central Catholic. All-boys school. Didn't want to start at a new school my senior year, but my dad got a job at Homestead Steel Works. So we had to move to Pittsburgh."

"I am going to go to a new school this year, too. What a coincidence!" Lilou said. Her face lit up at having something in common with Gary. Following Marianne's disappearance, her father had mentioned the possibility of sending Lilou to an all-girls high school, the Elizabeth School, but her mother resisted the idea. Now, in an instant, Lilou made the decision that she, too, would attend a new school in September. That way, she and Gary would have something in common.

"Really? Why?" Gary asked, opening his eyes wide. Lilou noticed they were a beautiful shade of blue.

"It's closer to here." Lilou shrugged.

"I see. Well, anyway, it was nice meeting you. I guess I'll see you around," Gary said.

"Bye." Lilou said and, elated, ran home.

"Your bag!" Gary called after her.

"Oh. Thank you." She turned around and grabbed the bag with butter, waving Gary goodbye.

After their first meeting, Lilou started dreaming of the handsome neighbor every night.

Their affair, as Lilou secretly referred to her obsession with the neighbor, was now in its second year. Now in her bedroom, as she waited for her mother to unpack so she could tell her the news of the accounting, Lilou thought fondly of that favorite memory – her first meeting with Gary. She loved thinking about how sweet Gary was when he asked her name, how kind and attentive he seemed.

In her dreams, they got to know each other, and Gary winked at her, took her hand in his, kissed her fingers, and professed his love for her. The scenes of their romance became steamier and steamier over time, but Lilou still reddened at the thought of Gary's face as he kissed her and pressed his body against hers.

Once in a dream, Gary confessed he wasn't ready for a proper relationship yet and she should wait a little while, and then everything between them would happen for sure. She just needed to turn twenty.

"I am counting the days, Linda," dream Gary told her. And so, Lilou waited. While she waited, she hadn't been to a single school dance, and had not confided in anyone about her love for Gary. Although she regularly saw him with other girls, Lilou remained faithful to her neighbor. But the reason for his dates with the others was because he wasn't yet ready for the pure, real love Lilou felt for him.

One day, he would be.

<hr>

Chapter 4
LARRY COLEMAN

<hr>

"Lilou! What kind of a surprise are we talking about here?" Her mother's voice interrupted Lilou's reverie.

"Maman, I am coming!" Lilou jumped off the bed and rushed downstairs. She found her mother standing in the living room, the open suitcase on the floor.

Lilou swallowed hard. Most of the time, interactions with her mother made her feel uncomfortable, as if her mother were looking for signs of her daughter's defectiveness. It could be Lilou's half-bitten nails, her mousy hair, or her love of math. Just about anything could set Katrine off, and then her mother would rant about how inadequate Lilou was.

"Lilou, please, just show it to me already!" Katrine demanded. "I am tired from the trip!"

"It's right here," Lilou said, her voice quiet. She bit her lower lip in nervous anticipation of her mother's reaction.

"Linda did the full accounting of your Mary Kay sales for the last twelve months," her father said. Lilou heard the steely notes in his voice. She knew the tone well. It was the one he used when his wife was being particularly hard on their daughter.

"Accounting?" Katrine snorted. "She's just a kid! What could she possibly understand? And besides, my papers were such a mess, there is no way she could make anything out." Her mother positioned herself on the sofa and crossed her legs beautifully. Katrine liked to make sure that her chiseled knees and slim ankles were accentuated.

"Katrine, take a look. Linda did a fantastic job!" Lilou's father repeated, standing next to his daughter.

"Can't this wait? I am exhausted!" Katrine pouted her lips.

"It will only take a minute." Her father handed his wife a folder Lilou had lovingly prepared. If Lilou didn't know any better, she would have guessed that her father was ready to start a fight. Katrine must have sensed the same thing, because she flicked the ash off her cigarette and reached for the papers. She opened the folder and examined its contents. Raising her eyebrows, she stared at the neat columns and rows of numbers in disbelief. Katrine scrutinized the numbers for several minutes, during which Lilou could barely breathe.

After a pause, her mother shrugged and nodded. That meant approval and gratitude. Lilou badly wished to hear actual words of approval, and her wish was granted.

"Did you do this all by yourself Lilou?" Katrine threw an incredulous look at her daughter.

Lilou noticed a smile on her father's face. "Yes." She blushed with pleasure at being noticed by her mother.

"That's quite something, chouchou[1]!" Lilou's heart leaped at the kind expression. Her mother hadn't used the term in ages.

"You see, Katrine, we have a genius in our family!" Michael Kelleher walked over to his daughter and gave her arm a gentle squeeze. Lilou felt tears well up in her eyes. This joint expression of love and approval from her parents was so rare. Her heart melted, and she was about to thank her parents when she heard her mother's voice.

"For a boy, this would have been quite useful. But for a girl? What's the point of all this intellectual rigor?" Katrine put the folder with the accounting papers aside and reached for another cigarette.

"Katrine, I am certain that our Linda here has a special talent. And we'll find a way for her to use it!"

"Michael, my only concern is Lilou's happiness. I hope she finds it," Katrine noted, staring across the room. "I want at least one of my girls to find joy in life." Her mother rolled the 'r' in the word 'girls', her French accent suddenly very heavy. Lilou felt an incredible sadness overcome her.

I am a failure, she thought.

Her mother's words reached her as if through a fog. "A woman is supposed to be beautiful, seductive, and attractive to men, not to be out there enjoying spreadsheets. Just think, if I were a math genius, you'd never have married me!" Katrine tilted her head and gave her husband a flirtatious wink.

"Our Linda has a great future ahead of her! You'll see!" Michael asserted, ignoring his wife's words.

"I wish she could just be a normal girl," Katrine added ruefully.

Lilou wanted to disappear, to fall right through the floor, to be as far away as possible from both of her parents. Her critical mother and her optimistic father.

Unable to stand it any longer, Lilou rushed out of the living room, tumbled down the porch stairs and dashed out onto the street. She ran, not thinking about where and why she was going. The only thing Lilou wanted at that moment was to be far away from her house. Tears welled up in her eyes, and she felt incredibly lonely and sad.

Shadyside was a beautiful, upscale part of town, with mansions, treelined streets, lush courtyards, manicured lawns and gardens. Lilou loved to wander the streets and look at the flowers. Most of all, she liked the hydrangeas that appeared in the gardens of the city in late spring and bloomed all through summer, some of them with a bluish tint, others with lilac undertones and soft pink coloring. But instead of enjoying the beautiful flowers, thoughts of anguish filled Lilou that afternoon, as she ran away from her house. *I could be like Marianne, I should just go off to California.*

She saw a small rock on the ground and kicked it. The rock hurt her toes, exposed in open sandals, and she yelped in pain. The pain made her stop. Lilou remembered how much she enjoyed sorting through her mother's papers, organizing the receipts, and then writing information down in neat columns. Reviewing the names of the customers and then imagining who they were based on their purchases was her favorite activity.

Immersed in those thoughts, Lilou gradually calmed down. She returned home in time for dinner. Neither her father nor her mother mentioned their afternoon flare-up, and all three of them pretended as if nothing happened. The evening passed in conversation about her mother's trip, who again delved into her sales, the genius of Mary Kay Ash, and about how deeply Katrine was impressed by the South.

The following morning, Michael Kelleher sat his daughter down at the kitchen table. He cleared his throat and looked down at his hands. Lilou was hungry, and she stared at the plate of waffles her mother had left for her, trying hard to pay attention despite the rumbling in her stomach. The smell of waffles was overpowering, and Lilou hoped the conversation would be a short one.

"Linda, princess," her father looked at her and then averted his eyes, "I've been thinking about something. I think you should become an accountant."

"Like your friend, Larry Coleman?" Lilou opened her eyes wide. Mr. Coleman was her father's close friend, a man in his late forties.

"Yes, princess," her father gave her a crooked smile.

"But Daddy, that's for men, isn't it?" Lilou tilted her head. She'd never heard of a woman working as an accountant.

"Oh, I don't think so. I'll ask Larry. I think they take women these days. You know, the world is changing." Michael Kelleher looked at his daughter carefully.

"So I'll work in an office?"

"Yes, Linda." Her father was silent for a moment. He put down his fork. "It'll be good for you to be independent. In case, you know."

"Daddy? What do you mean?" Forgetting about the waffles and her hunger, Lilou stared at him.

"Well, princess, it's good to have options. And you never know, with the conversation we had with your mother, it got me thinking. And I do think that with your abilities, you really should have a profession." Her father picked up the fork and started eating.

Lilou knew that there were several career tracks women could have. A nurse, a teacher, or a librarian. Lilou couldn't stand the sight of blood, so nursing was not for her, and while she loved books, she did not like them enough to dedicate her whole life to them as a librarian. That left teaching. Since she liked math, Lilou assumed she would teach mathematics. It made perfect sense. Becoming an accountant did not. In reality, Lilou did not expect to work. Not for long. Lilou pictured herself in the role of Gary's wife, sitting on the couch in their living room and waiting for him to come home, handsome, tall, and in love with her. She immediately blushed at the thought.

"But Daddy, why an accountant? I thought I'd teach math or something."

"I was thinking, Larry, he can help. You know, we served together, so I think he can tell you what you need to do to become an accountant. He's got a CPA. I think once he understands how perfect you are for that type of work, he'll hire you himself!" Michael Kelleher gave Lilou a reassuring smile.

"Sure, Daddy," Lilou forced herself to agree. She did not like contradicting her father. *Maybe it won't be so bad? And anyway, it'll only be until Gary and I have children.* Lilou thought, as she reached for the waffles and, salivating, took the first delicious bite.

A few weeks later, Larry Coleman appeared in their living room. Katrine, though she'd opposed the idea of Lilou becoming an accountant, prepared snacks for their guest and forced Lilou to wear a new dress for the occasion.

"But it doesn't matter what I wear!" Lilou protested, as her mother forced her into a peach-colored dress with a bow. "I am going to learn about accounting! Who cares what I look like?"

"You never know! A woman should always look her best, and especially a young girl!" Katrine gave her a doubtful look. Lilou felt miserable in her new outfit. She hated the color, hated how it made her skin look corpse-like, but her mother insisted that the pinkish undertones were 'refreshing' and tied the bow around her waist. Lilou cautiously descended the stairs to find her father and Larry Coleman toasting their friendship in the living room.

Lilou's father was in his favorite spot, on the couch, while Larry sat in the armchair next to him.

"There is she, my Linda. All grown up!" Michael Kelleher said, his voice tainted with nervousness. "So, as I was telling you, Larry, Linda here is great at math. I mean, sharp, she's got a real talent. The other day she did the numbers for Katrine, got all her Mary Kay sales for a whole year added up. So," Lilou's father scratched his chin, "I was thinking maybe she could consider becoming an accountant. What do you say?" He looked at Larry Coleman quizzically.

"An accountant? A girl? I don't know, Mike, that'll be the first one!" Larry shook his head and then frowned.

"You mean there aren't any women in your firm?"

"I mean, sure, there are girls, but they are all secretaries," Larry rolled his eyes, "so, you know."

"But the real accountants, no women? Not even one?" Michael Kelleher stared at his friend.

"You see! I knew it!" Katrine appeared from the kitchen, holding a cigarette and shook her head in disapproval. "Michael, this is a crazy idea!"

"Wait, Katrine, hold on for a second." Lilou's father turned to his friend. "But women aren't forbidden from joining the firm, are they?"

"No, of course not, I heard in our Chicago office, we got a woman, joined a few years ago. But here, in Pittsburgh, we just don't have any suitable candidates. I never thought about it."

"So, theoretically, it's possible?" Michael Kelleher insisted.

"Sure, sure, I guess so."

"That's great!" Michael shifted in his seat. "So what does Linda have to do? Major in accounting in college? Linda can do it. She's a smart girl." Her father gave his daughter a look full of pride, and she wanted to disappear, so ashamed she was of being the center of attention.

"Mike," Larry paused and frowned. "I am just thinking. Let's say she gets the job, we got business trips. Long hours. We travel all the time, you know that, part of the job, and then is she going to travel with the men? Stay in a hotel with us? What about the spouses? What's my wife going to say if she finds out I am traveling with a woman?"

"Oh, Larry, but can't she maybe not travel? And maybe by the time Linda here starts at your firm, there will be other women, too?" Michael Kelleher looked at his friend hopefully.

"Maybe." Larry sighed.

"Michael, I can't imagine," Katrine intervened again. "Our girl, her reputation!"

"Katrine, please, Linda is no fool!" Michael Kelleher threw a disgruntled look at his wife. "Is there any more shrimp? We're all out." He pointed at the empty plate.

Katrine rolled her eyes, grabbed the plate and strode into the kitchen, her whole body showing resentment.

What do I do? Lilou panicked. *How will I ever work with all men? And what if my Gary feels jealous? If I work as a teacher, he won't care, there it's mostly women, but if I become an accountant?*

Thoughts of Gary and their life together absorbed the rest of the afternoon, and Lilou barely noticed Larry Coleman's departure and that fact that her fate was sealed. She would one day become an accountant.

Chapter 5
THE WEDDING INVITATION

April 22nd, 1973

The countdown was over. Lilou had impatiently waited for her twentieth birthday to come, after which she knew she would blossom. She and Gary would be together. Their love would be nothing like anything she'd ever experienced before. It would be explosive, beautiful, blinding in its passion.

Time flew by unnoticed, perforated only by her daily countdowns of the time remaining. Lilou went to Pitt, majored in accounting, and continued living at home. She was the only girl in her major, and shied away from socializing at college. Lilou had no close friends, but that didn't trouble her. Cordial to her peers, she excelled academically. Her junior year was nearly finished. As before, she read at night, only it was mostly accounting textbooks. She continued dreaming of Gary, his handsome face, and their future together.

Gary was away, studying at Penn State. There was no talk of Gary's graduation, and Lilou suspected this was due to his trying to avoid being drafted for Vietnam. Since the end of the Vietnam draft had been announced in January of that year, much to the chagrin of her father, Lilou expected Gary to come back soon. Whenever he came home during breaks from college, she made sure they 'ran into each other' at least every other day. Gary was always friendly and they would chit chat and even joke together. Lilou never felt shy around him. When he went back to Penn State, she missed her neighbor terribly, but the thought of their strong connection that prevailed despite the distance comforted her.

As her father had suggested, she majored in accounting and loved every minute of it. Studying came easily and she got good grades. Accounting delighted her in every way, and confirmed Lilou's understanding of the basic axiom in life: there was a balance in everything. Accounts payables had to match accounts receivable. That comforted Lilou. No matter what, in the end, both columns had to add up. Debit and credit. It was all so simple and beautiful. Lilou also thought that she would never actually work as an accountant. She would get married right after college and become a homemaker. Gary would work, while she would stay home.

She never mentioned her plans to her father. Lilou knew he would never approve of what she intended to do. He had envisioned a glorious future for his daughter. From time to time, Larry Coleman would appear at their home and discussions about Pedersen Accountants would occur. Lilou paid little attention to them. It would all happen only once she graduated from college, and by then she would be happily paired off with Gary.

With every grade 'A' Lilou brought home, her father reaffirmed the notion that his daughter would become 'the best accountant in all of Pittsburgh'. Then it became 'all of Western Pennsylvania', and when Lilou was about to finish her junior year with a 3.9 GPA, it was 'the best accountant in all of America'.

On the day of her twentieth birthday, Lilou woke up in a great mood. *Zero to countdown!* She thought. She'd made it to the most magical day of her life. She stretched and headed downstairs. It was a Friday, and she had only one class. Her father had already left for work, and her mother was on the phone, speaking to one of her Mary Kay clients.

By then, Katrine Kelleher was traveling almost every day to meetings and tea parties to sell Mary Kay cosmetics. How Katrine had time to plan these gatherings, how she found new clients, how she built relationships with them, all that was shrouded in mystery, but in the nearly five years since her mother began selling Mary Kay cosmetics, her clientele has grown and expanded beyond Pittsburgh. Katrine now had adorable pink business cards, and their house overflowed with boxes and packages of cosmetics, awaiting new customers. Her mother stored most of them in Marianne's old bedroom, which had become known as 'the office', but often, when there were new deliveries, she would leave boxes lying around in the living room, much to the dismay of Lilou's father.

Katrine Kelleher was happy. She radiated exuberance, adoring the creams and lotions, memorizing the ingredients by heart. Lilou's mother had developed a deep understanding of how each product affected the skin of her clients. She could talk for hours about their magical properties, about moisturizers, about lipstick and how to properly apply it, how to use the powder and the eyebrow pencil just right.

When Katrine hosted Mary Kay parties at their house, Lilou would find her mother surrounded by customers, watching in awe, as her mother extolled Mary Kay, applying the latest product with the skill of a magician. Katrine dreamed of a pink Cadillac, which Mary Kay Ash gifted to the most successful consultants. Each summer in July, she traveled to Texas for the Mary Kay convention, and came back inspired, brimming with ideas and plans on how to boost sales. Lilou had been doing her mother's accounting since that first summer – a challenging task, but they had settled into a routine, and Lilou was now firmly in charge of everything.

Her mother often forgot her customers' names, but she never ever forgot a face. It was easier for Katrine to remember their appearances and what they bought than the method of payment or where her clients lived. Knowing her mother's lack of organization, soon after doing the first spreadsheet with the Mary Kay sales, Lilou bought her a pink notebook and asked Katrine to enter sales information there.

"Maman, I am thinking, maybe you can write down what someone bought right after it happens?" Lilou said, averting her eyes. She was embarrassed when speaking with her mother about Mary Kay. Lilou felt as if her very being was not worthy of her mother's business. She, Lilou, was too unattractive, too awkward, so that even being allowed to handle her mother's accounting was a miracle in itself.

"Oh, yes, of course," Katrine hummed, as she accepted the pink notebook from her daughter and flipped it in her hands. Lilou had spent hours at a stationary store, trying to make sure the color and the size were perfect and fit her mother's taste. She expected her mother to notice and to compliment her on the notebook, but Katrine merely nodded and tucked it in her purse. The following week, Lilou nudged her mother and asked to see the notebook, anticipating neat rows of sales entries. Opening the first page, she saw the first entry: "Blonde, bow-legged, lipstick and moisturizer."

"Maman, do you have the name of the customer? Did she pay by check or cash?"

"The name? Starts with an 'S', I think." Katrine gave her daughter a confused look.

"What was the total?" Lilou felt tears well up in her eyes. Her plan to organize her mother's sales was failing in front of her very eyes.

"Who cares? I got the money. What does it matter?" Katrine shrugged. "Oh, wait, her name is Louise."

"And the last name?" Lilou looked up at her mother with renewed hope.

"Simpson? Or Smith? I think there was an 'S' there somewhere." Katrine took a cigarette out of the case and lit it.

"Maman, could you please write down their name and address next time?" Lilou swallowed hard. She hoped that her voice did not sound shrill, but she felt exhaustion and hopelessness. She'd been working tirelessly to help her mother. All of her efforts were being wasted.

"I knew it! I should have asked a real professional to help me! But I gave you a chance and listened to your father. How silly of me?" Katrine sighed and puffed on the cigarette.

"I am sorry, Maman. I'm just trying to help." Lilou responded, choking back tears. She loved her mother and she loved accounting. Helping her mother with Mary Kay combined her two loves, but all of her good intentions were going unnoticed.

"You know what would help me? If you didn't bother me with these silly details. I help women become more beautiful. That's my business. I am not a numbers person!" Katrine pointed her toe and wiggled her foot, as she always did in times of distress. Lilou was about to run away in tears, but at that moment, her father walked into the living room.

"How are my girls doing?" Michael Kelleher's voice boomed. He quickly glanced at Lilou, noticing the disappointed expression on her face, and turned to his wife. Immediately, Katrine raised her eyebrows. She knew her husband would take their daughter's side and ended the conversation. The pink notebook stayed and, with time, Katrine Kelleher started recording sales with more care and effort.

THE MORNING of her twentieth birthday, on the kitchen table, Lilou saw her favorite breakfast, waffles with maple syrup. She could smell the caramelized apples and guessed that her mother was planning on making Tarte Tatin as her birthday cake. Katrine hung up the receiver and walked into the kitchen.

"Happy birthday, chouchou!" her mother said and kissed Lilou on the cheek.

"Thank you, Maman!" Lilou smiled at her mother, her heart filling with gratitude. Her twentieth birthday was turning out to be a wonderful day. Lilou quickly finished her waffles and decided to go outside. The weather was beautiful, the birds were chirping, and Lilou wanted to take in the fresh air, the blooming flowers. The world felt on her side.

"Go ahead, Lilou." Katrine gave her a nod and turned her attention to making the dessert.

Lilou rushed outside. She threw a look at Gary's house, as she usually did, and thought of her beloved, not expecting to see him. She turned and suddenly, there he was! Gary was walking up the street. She froze in place. It could not have been him. He was away in college. But the vision got closer. Gary was very real, and was carrying a gallon of milk.

"Hey there, Linda," Gary said.

Lilou noticed how the muscles of his right arm flexed as he gripped the milk, and how well the t-shirt with the Penn State Nittany lion mascot accentuated his torso. Lilou felt as if the lion was watching her, and she felt uneasy under its gaze.

"Hi," Lilou said and blushed. Seeing Gary on her birthday was a good omen. She felt her heart leap. *It's happening so fast!* Lilou thought. *Fate!* "Today is my birthday!" Lilou said, before she could stop herself.

"Happy birthday!" A smirk appeared on his face.

"Thank you." Lilou's mind immediately drifted to thoughts of the kinds of presents Gary would give her for her birthday once they were married. *Maybe a necklace? Or a pair of earrings?*

"I heard you're studying accounting. That's cool! We don't have many girls at Penn State. And especially not in accounting! Mostly, they are out there to get an MRS. degree, if you know what I mean," Gary winked at her.

"Yeah," Lilou managed to squeeze out. She hated attracting attention to her academic achievements.

"So, are you gonna be a teacher?" Gary raised his eyebrows.

"I don't know," Lilou said in a near whisper. She felt shivers run down her spine. *Gary is about to ask me on a date.* The thought flashed in her mind. Lilou adjusted her hair. This was the moment she'd been waiting for, and she needed to look good.

"You got a boyfriend?" Gary asked. In response, Lilou turned beet red. For nearly five years, she'd been waiting for their conversations to progress to this new level!

"No," Lilou averted her gaze and looked at the ground, as she'd seen women do in soap operas. That's how women acted during confessions of love.

"Oh, that's 'cause you probably don't have time for guys. My girlfriend never went to college. We're getting married this summer! In August. She's been planning our wedding for months. It seems to be taking her a lot of time. I don't know how she'd be able to do it if she was studying. But Samantha's not into that stuff." Gary shrugged, showing that everything in his girlfriend suited him just fine.

"Girlfriend?" Lilou swallowed hard. Gary's words did not fully penetrate her consciousness. *Did Gary just mention someone named Samantha?*

"Yeah, Sammy. My girlfriend. Anyway, I gotta run, mom's waiting for the milk. But you should come to the wedding. I'll tell Samantha to put you on the guest list. I'm sure my parents will invite yours anyway. The ceremony will be at our church," Gary pointed somewhere at a distance.

"Church," Lilou mumbled. She felt like she was about to throw up. She couldn't breathe. With every passing second, Lilou knew she was moving closer to death.

"Yeah, St Regis, right here in Shadyside. Hope to see you there. Sammy will like you. She's, you know, not too bright, but she loves smart people!" A fond smile crossed Gary's face.

"Sammy?" Lilou tried to hold back tears that were now welling up in her eyes.

"Yeah, Samantha. But I like to call her Sammy. I think it's cute. She loves it!"

"Congratulations!" Lilou forced herself to say and, unable to wait for an answer, ran home.

Chapter 6
THE MELTDOWN

Gulping down tears, she ran into her house.

"Is that you, Lilou?" She heard her mother's voice. "Why are you back so soon? Is it too cold outside?"

Unable to answer, Lilou doubled over, her legs buckled underneath her. A low sound came up from the pit of her stomach. It was a howl. The kind a wounded animal makes. She ran upstairs, leaping two steps at a time. Bang. Lilou slammed her bedroom door shut and threw herself on the bed. She wept. Angry, ferocious tears. Her body convulsed in sobs. Lilou buried her face in the pillow, trying hard to stop the wave of emotion. She could not remember ever crying so hard in her life.

Gary. She called the name of her beloved, wishing for him to console her. *How could he? Gary is about to marry someone else. Why is this happening? Today of all days. Who is Samantha?* At the thought of Gary marrying another woman, Lilou cried even harder. She pictured the gentle smile that crossed his face as he mentioned his fiancée and bitter tears flooded her eyes. *Sammy! He even has an adorable nickname for her! We never had a chance!* Bile rose in her throat as she imagined Sammy with a blonde ponytail, giggling and winking mischievously at Gary. *And I am so dumb! How did I let this happen?*

"Lilou!" There was a knock on the door. She did not answer. Pressing the pillow to her face, she tried to stifle her sobs. There was no use going on. *What future do I have without my beloved Gary?* Another knock on the door. "Can I come in?" Her mother's voice, muffled by the pillow, barely reached her ears. Instead of an answer, Lilou positioned the pillow over her face, hoping it would hide her tear-stricken face.

"Get up." Her mother's voice was now closer. It sounded urgent.

"Umm," Lilou squeezed out.

"Please get up. Let's have some cake. I finished Tarte Tatin. Your favorite." Katrine sat on the bed and patted Lilou's shoulder.

"I am not hungry," Lilou responded through the pillow.

"What kind of woman acts like this?" Her mother tried to gently pry the pillow from her face, but Lilou resisted.

"I dunno." Fresh tears rolled down her face, and Lilou convulsed in another wave of sobs. A sharp pain pierced her. Her dream, the love of her life, the reason for her very existence, had betrayed her. Gary was marrying someone else and she would be alone forever.

"Please remember, no man is worth your tears. Ever! No man in the world!" Lilou could tell that her mother rose from the bed and was pacing the room. "Men are there for us women, to pay for things and to love and adore us. Not the other way around. And if you cry over a man, it means that he doesn't love you. And if that's the case, you shouldn't waste your emotions on him!" Katrine stomped her foot.

"How do you know?" Lilou slowly removed the pillow and sat up on her bed. Her mother had never spoken to Lilou about relationships and men before. It piqued Lilou's interest.

"How do I know what?" Katrine scanned her daughter's face.

"That I am crying over a maaaan." The corners of Lilou's mouth drooped and Lilou felt another pang of sadness. *Gary! Gary*! Lilou pushed the now soaking wet pillow back over her face and slammed her head down on the bed.

"Lilou, please, chouchou." Her mother leaned over her, gently pushing the pillow aside to reveal Lilou's red and puffy face. "What else could a young dummy like you cry about?" Katrine said, her tone softer.

Lilou convulsed in a sob, but the moment of crisis had passed. "But we were meant to be together!" Lilou sighed.

"Chouchou, if you are meant to be together, it will all work out on its own. Just like me and your father." Katrine sighed. "Why don't you get yourself together, it's your birthday. And you have class today, don't you?"

"Yes." Lilou sat up once more. She'd forgotten all about college. "I have to get ready." It was almost noon. "Thank you, Maman." Lilou got off the bed and went to the bathroom. Seeing her face in the mirror, she gasped. Streaks of tears crisscrossed her cheeks. Her eyes were bright red, and her eyelids were swollen. Her nose was beet-red and her hair looked like a bird's nest.

"Maman, I don't think I can go out like this," Lilou said. There was no answer.

Lilou peeked out, but her mother had gone downstairs. She felt a fresh wave of tears come. *Gary. Gary!* Lilou rose and walked to the window, pulling back the curtain. She caught herself thinking, but then remembered that he would soon marry someone else. Her whole life plan had imploded, and she did not know what to do with her life. The dream of being a homemaker, happily coupled with Gary had disappeared in a flash. Lilou fell back on the bed and wept.

The familiar walls of her bedroom looked strange and foreign. Lilou had no more strength to get up, so she rolled over and covered her head with the blanket, pushing the damp pillow out of the way. Suddenly she heard a squeak. Lilou pulled the blanket back and saw a pair of eyes staring back at her. They looked unmistakably human, only the human they belonged to had to be tiny. Lilou fidgeted slightly, then rubbed her eyes to wipe the tears away. When she opened them again, the strange vision was gone.

"Please, get up, Lilou." She heard her mother's voice. Lilou did not know how much time had passed. "It's time to go to Pitt. I brought up some make-up. It's a new line Mary Kay just introduced." There was a clicking sound and Lilou could hear her mother put something heavy on the floor.

Lilou had often wondered when she did her mother's accounting what it would be like to use the Mary Kay products, such as mascara, eyeliner, lipstick, and all the rest. But she had no strength to move.

"Lilou." She felt her mother's hand on her shoulder. In response, Lilou shook her head and closed her eyes. Sleep offered a consolation.

She dreamed of Gary. He kissed her face, told her he was sorry and that they would soon be together. *Gary!* Lilou yelled out and woke up to the sound of her own scream. And then she remembered. *He is marrying someone else.* Her whole body hurt. Her head was pulsating as she sat up and her lips felt parched. She thought of doing the countdown to her twentieth birthday, but then remembered that she had already turned twenty. *It's zero. Zero,* she thought. *I have no reason to go on.* She fell back onto the bed.

When Lilou opened her eyes again, it was dark outside. She saw her father standing by the door. Lilou stayed curled on her bed. She felt numb.

"Linda, honey," her father cleared his throat. She heard him sit on the chair opposite her bed. Lilou didn't stir. "Umm, princess, I… I want to talk to you." Michael Kelleher, normally energetic and quick to take action, paused. After a moment of hesitation, he pulled the chair closer to her bed. She felt his hand rest on her shoulder through the blanket. "Can you hear me?" Lilou moved her foot, which indicated that she was listening. "Linda, it's your birthday. Please come. Let's have some cake." Silence. Her father waited by her bed and then left, closing the door behind him.

Lilou did not remember what happened next. She lost count of the days, settling into a routine. She didn't get out of bed. Her father would come in first thing every morning, greeting her and speaking to her before leaving for work. Her mother would then take Lilou to the bathroom, sitting Lilou in the bathtub to wipe her with a sponge. Once a week, her mother washed her hair. The rest of the time, Lilou spent in bed in a catatonic state. Her mother appeared with trays of food that Lilou barely touched. She had no appetite.

She had strange visions of a bird. It was a crow, and it would tap on her window every morning without fail. The crow, perched right outside her window, waited until Lilou opened her eyes, then tilted its head, let out a cackle, and flew away. The same vision repeated each day, but was so fantastical that Lilou wasn't sure whether the bird was real or imaginary.

One afternoon, she heard muffled voices outside the door.

"Please, right this way, doctor." Her father opened the door and an unfamiliar smell filled the room. Cologne mixed with something clinical. The combination irritated her nose. Lilou sneezed.

"Hello there, Linda." She heard a deep baritone. "I am Doctor Fleming. I am a psychiatrist. Your father tells me you aren't feeling well."

Lilou pulled the blanket over her head, covering her face for security. *If I wait long enough, he will leave.* She wanted the man to disappear, so she could go back to her routine of staying in bed.

"Linda, let me feel your pulse," the doctor said, his tone firm. Lilou felt cold fingers on her wrist and jerked it away.

"You see, I, I can't stand it." Her mother's voice sounded shrill, as if she was on the verge of tears. "Doctor, she just lays there all day."

"Katrine, please." Lilou heard her father.

"That's why I am here, Mrs. Kelleher. Please, don't worry. I can help your daughter. In a case like this, I recommend electric shock therapy. It can do miracles," Dr. Fleming said, his smell moving away from the bed. His words reached Lilou, but she did not care.

"What? Where?" There were hysterical notes in Katrine's voice. *Maman is worried,* Lilou thought and closed her eyes.

"Electric shock? Are you going to take Linda in?" Michael Kelleher asked. "Isn't there anything else that could be done?"

"Shock treatment is a wonderful, proven treatment. It works wonders." The baritone noted. "I can get everything organized for you in no time."

"Thank you, Doctor." The voices retreated from the room.

Lilou heard the door close. She pulled the blanket off her head. The psychiatrist's smell lingered and Lilou forced herself to get up and go to the bathroom. There, she vomited. *I am dying.* A thought flashed through her mind. *Gary killed me. Zero, Zero,* she thought, and then collapsed back on the bed. The end was near, Lilou could feel it. If she did not get up from her bed for a few more days, she would simply disappear, dissolve into the abyss. *No more pain.*

Lilou woke up to the sun beaming through the curtains. Only when she sat up on the bed did she see that both of her parents were standing in the room. Her mother's hands were on her hips.

"Lilou, good to see you are awake," her mother said.

"Linda." Her father sat on the chair by the bed. "Your mother and I, we talked about what to do." Her father looked up at his wife and then at Lilou, who sat motionless. "Princess, can you please look at me?" As she did, a gentle smile appeared on his face. "Good. So, princess, we decided to send you to France this summer. The decision wasn't easy for us, but we love you. And we don't want you to get shock treatment."

"Yes, chouchou, you will be traveling to Paris." Her mother added.

"France?" Lilou gasped and stared at her parents. It was her first word spoken in days, and she noticed that her parents exchanged glances.

Visiting France had been a near-taboo topic. "My life is here now," her mother would say. She never mentioned anything about her childhood, except for the fact that she had grown up in Paris, which Katrine noted only when pointing out the provincial elements of their Pittsburgh life.

France was a place that was superior culturally, but otherwise out of reach. Lilou had always assumed that her mother's reticence was due to the trauma of World War II that her father experienced while serving in France, and that her mother was being careful of her father's feelings.

"Yes, princess, I got your ticket already." Her father gave her a reassuring smile.

"But how would I go?" Lilou's mouth gaped open. The prospect of a flight to France sounded unrealistic, irrational. Like traveling to the moon.

"It's okay, princess, you will be fine. You have family there. Your grandparents. They are waiting for you," he said.

"Grand-mère?" Lilou stared at her mother. Grand-mère Régine was mentioned only once a year, when they received Christmas cards from her. Lilou had never seen her photos and knew little about the woman.

"Yes, Grand-mère Régine and Grand-père Guillaume," Katrine said, biting her lip. "Why don't you get up and we can talk about everything downstairs?"

Without saying another word, her father rose from the chair and exited the room. Lilou's mother followed. As they closed the door behind them, Lilou heard him whisper: "You see, it's working!"

Lilou rose from the bed. Her head spun, and she had to lean on the bed frame to stabilize herself. She got dressed, for the first time in days, picking out her clothes. They hung loosely on her body, and she realized that she must have lost weight. In the mirror, the reflection staring back at her was gaunt. Her cheeks were sunken in and her hair hung in dull streaks. Lilou sighed and headed downstairs.

There, she found her parents sitting next to each other at the kitchen table. Her mother was twisting a near-empty porcelain cup in her hands, while her father drummed his fingers.

"Ah! There she is!" Michael Kelleher clapped, seeing Lilou appear. "Have a seat, Linda, please." He pointed to a chair, where Lilou usually occupied. As she sat down, she felt her stomach rumbling and realized she felt hungry.

"Linda, we love you and want you to get better. We thought that going to France would be a good idea. You can connect with your family there. A change of scenery," her father said.

"Yes, you'll then go stay with Auntie Monique. She lives in Lyon. And you've got cousins there," Katrine added.

"Auntie Monique? Who is that?" Lilou felt her head spin.

"My sister, Monique. And her daughter Aline. Your cousin. She must be sixteen or seventeen now. And I think there is also a boy." Katrine shrugged and reached for a cigarette. "Monique married well. She lives in a nice part of Lyon, so you can stay with them for a few days."

"You have a sister in Lyon?" Lilou had no recollection of her mother ever mentioning having a sister.

"Yes, didn't I ever tell you about her?" Katrine opened her eyes wide.

"Princess, you'll see a bit of France." Michael Kelleher smiled. Katrine sucked in her breath. "And you'll get away from here for a bit. We think a change of scenery will do you good."

Lilou stared at her parents, unable to speak.

France. I am going to France!

Chapter 7
PREPARATIONS

The following morning, Lilou woke up to her mother standing in her bedroom.

"Time to get up, Lilou, we are going shopping!" Katrine said. She was wearing a beautiful light pink dress, with a long slit, which accentuated her long legs.

"Right now?" Lilou mumbled, rubbing her eyes. Her mother nodded, and Lilou slowly rose from the bed and hobbled to the bathroom.

"Your father is heading to the travel agency, and you and I need to buy you a suitcase and a whole new wardrobe." Katrine gave Lilou an appraising stare. "You are going to have to look your best!"

"Travel agency? I thought Daddy already got the ticket." Lilou stared at her mother.

"No, of course not, we were just testing the waters yesterday. To see if you were in a condition to travel."

"What?" Lilou gasped and stared at her mother's reflection in the bathroom mirror. Lilou thought she saw a smirk on her mother's face. "So, I am not going to France?"

"Katrine cleared her throat. "You are! But chouchou," her mother had been using the endearing term more often, ever since Lilou's twentieth birthday, "your father and I had no idea if you would get out of bed. Let alone agree to travel to France."

"So, what would have happened if I didn't agree to go?" Lilou put her hand to her mouth. She felt tears well up in her eyes.

"I don't know. I suppose we might have had to take you to that awful doctor."

"Maman!" Lilou gasped.

"But it's fine now. You'll travel to France, it's definitely the solution. Please, Lilou, wash your face," Katrine ordered, all signs of tenderness gone from her voice. Sounding like the stern mother Lilou knew all of her childhood.

Cold water made her feel better for a brief moment, but then she was back to feeling sad and pitiful. Lilou turned around and faced her mother.

"I don't want to leave!" Lilou whimpered. All she wanted to do was to crawl back into bed, cover her face with the pillow and cry again. Fresh tears welled up in her eyes and she felt an incredible sadness over her lost dream. Gary was never going to be her husband, and she would spend her whole life alone, a sad accountant.

"Lilou. I am the last person to want to send you to France. Believe me. But your father and I think a change of scenery will do you good." Katrine sighed.

"But why? I want to stay here! I will be fine." Lilou pleaded. "What about college? I have to finish the year!"

"That will have to wait until the fall. Your father spoke to them, and Pitt agreed to have you take the exams in September," Katrine said.

"So I didn't fail the semester?" Lilou opened her eyes wide. While suffering over Gary and her crushed dreams, she did not once think of accounting, her grades or the university. But now she felt jittery with worry over her degree.

"No. You can thank Daddy later. Lilou, please, enough. You'll be back from France in three weeks!" Katrine tapped her foot on the floor, a sign of her impatience. "Please get ready, I don't have much time. I've got client appointments in the afternoon, I am invited to a bridal shower."

At the mention of a bridal shower, she remembered Gary and Sammy and collapsed on the bed, sobbing. The thought of their happiness cut like a knife.

"Chouchou, please, don't cry." Katrine leaned over her and petted her head. Her mother was once again, kind and tender, and Lilou melted at her mother's touch.

"I can't ever leave the house!" Lilou cried out, burying her face in her mother's lap.

"Lilou, remember, when you were a little girl? Do you remember how we sat like this, you and I?" Katrine asked. She was moving her hand gently over Lilou's head, and Lilou's tears slowly receded.

"Nooo," Lilou sobbed. She tried, but could not remember any expressions of tenderness and love from her mother. Instead, she could only recall her mother's stern looks, judgment, cruelty even.

"Oh, yes, you were three years old, and you loved listening to stories. You'd get on my lap and I would read you fairy tales. Cinderella and Little Red Riding Hood. You loved that one! And you know who your favorite character was?"

"Nooo," Lilou answered, perking up her ears. The recollection of her childhood by her mother was giving her a fresh perspective. *Was there something to my story that I may have missed?*

"The wolf! It was the wolf! The wolf from the Little Red Riding Hood." Katrine clapped her hands and howled with laughter.

"What?" Lilou sat up and stared at her mother.

"Yes, you felt sorry for the wolf and he was your hero. Can you believe it? You even wanted a stuffed animal, a wolf, as a toy. We managed to find one, and then you dressed him like a grandmother and played with him."

"I don't remember any of this." Lilou shrugged. A part of her wished to return to those days, when she was young and innocent, and enthralled in the story of Little Red Riding Hood, to relive the magic of her childhood. But all Lilou could remember now was how she'd been counting down to the age of twenty.

"You used to sleep with that toy wolf!" Katrine exclaimed. "I think we have him somewhere in the attic." Her mother smiled at Lilou and then pursed her lips. "But now, please get ready, so we can go shopping." Katrine rose from the bed and impatiently tapped her foot.

"But what's the point?" Lilou threw a hopeless look at her mother.

"What's the point? Are you a woman or a sack of potatoes?" Katrine exclaimed and rolled her eyes. "As a woman, you have to do your best to look great. It's just part of life!"

"No one cares!"

"How would you know that? If you are always hiding or living in a dream, you'll never know."

Her mother's words cut like a knife. *How does she know about my dreams?* Lilou's heart sank.

"You'll miss all the possibilities in life! If I hadn't gone to that dance, I wouldn't have met your father." Katrine scanned her daughter's face for a reaction. "And remember, it's the woman who chooses a man! I should have had this talk with you earlier, but I just didn't think you were interested. It seems like I missed something." Her mother straightened her dress and gave her daughter the relentless look of a person who was not used to losing. "Nothing like shopping to make you feel good!" Katrine added after a pause, and Lilou sighed in defeat. "I'll make us some coffee. Your father should bring back your tickets this afternoon!" Katrine turned around and left the room, and Lilou heard the clicking of her mother's heels on the parquet floor.

The rest of the week was a blur. Lilou went shopping with her mother, not once, as she expected, but every day, comparing different suitcases, trying on new dresses and shoes, and even doing a fitting for a skirt that her mother found in her closet and decided that Lilou had to take with her to France. A part of Lilou reveled in the newfound attention from her mother, and enjoyed spending time together. But the fittings, the obsequious comments from the sales associates, discussions about the virtues of a pink dress versus a blue one, demonstrations of the latest and the most exclusive styles, and, inevitably, her mother's promotion of Mary Kay cosmetics on the sidelines, made Lilou grow weary.

By the end of the week, equipped with several new outfits and two sturdy yet stylish suitcases that 'would last a lifetime', she was done. When, at the end of the week, her mother announced 'just one last trip to the store', Lilou shook her head. Sitting at the kitchen table, Lilou put her fork down.

"No, please, Maman, I can't take it anymore!" Lilou knew she sounded ungrateful. The week that she'd spent in the company of her mother had done wonders for her self-esteem, and had eased her suffering over Gary's nuptials.

"Lilou, just one more trip! You are flying out tomorrow!"

"I can't do this anymore, please!" Lilou begged.

"Lilou, you are absolutely coming to the store. We need to try on that yellow dress. They were supposed to change the zipper. Don't you remember?" Katrine sighed. "I don't understand why I care more about your outfits than you do! You are the one who needs to worry about these things. Don't you care about your looks?"

With her mother's question, it was as if the world had stopped. *Do I care about my looks?* Now that the question was asked of her, she did not have an answer.

"I, I don't know," Lilou mumbled and felt her cheeks turn red. *Do I care?* She definitely wanted to look good and to be attractive, but she always assumed that her looks were too plain for that. It was her inner beauty that would shine and then the right person would appreciate it. And that one person would be Gary, her one true love. Gary was the one who'd noticed her, who'd see through her mousy exterior. She had been so lucky as to find him early on, so Lilou did not have to look attractive to other men. But now that Gary was getting married to the treacherous Sammy, Lilou no longer knew what to do.

"Well, I think you do! And I can help you improve your appearance. I should have done it a long time ago, I really should have." Katrine sighed again and her face took on a regretful expression. "But it was all those books you were reading, and then Marianne ran away, and I just was so depressed. I am sorry." Her mother's hand shook slightly, as she poured herself coffee spilling a little on table.

"I am sorry too, Maman." Not knowing how to react

to her mother's words, Lilou apologized back, and rushed to wipe the spilled coffee with a napkin.

"Maybe now I can make it up to you. I can show you how to use Mary Kay, and the clothes. I think you'll be alright. And I have to tell you one more thing, umm," Katrine cleared her throat and looked away. "You will be meeting with Grand-mère. I must warn you, Lilou, be careful with your grandmother. Don't fall under her influence."

"What do you mean?" Lilou stared. Her mother's voice had a note of urgency, something more than just a warning. As if real danger lay ahead.

"How can I put it?" Katrine averted her gaze and stared blankly at the cup of coffee. "You see, your grandmother is an unusual person. You'll see for yourself. She can be very charming, very convincing, and you just have to know where to draw the line."

"The line?" Lilou felt a lump form in her throat. Even a trip to France, which she'd finally started to view as a respite from her suffering, might have its own pitfalls in the form of her grandmother.

"I am confident that you'll be fine. You have your head on your shoulders, you are a smart girl, and you are twenty years old! Just use your judgment, you can tell right from wrong! I am just worried for nothing." Katrine rambled on, as if speaking would dilute the gravity of her words.

"Don't worry, Maman." Lilou forced a smile, feeling shivers run down her spine.

"Very good, very good, so this evening I am going to show you a few Mary Kay creams and teach you how to apply make-up." Katrine gave her daughter a gentle squeeze.

That very evening, Katrine sat Lilou down in front of the vanity in the master bathroom and for three hours lectured her daughter on various creams, lotions, their applications, color combinations for make-up, lipstick, eyeshadow, and mascara. Lilou tried to take notes, but her mother laughed at her attempts, telling Lilou that, "Beauty has to be felt, not learned".

By the end of the evening, Lilou felt tired and confused. The only thing she remembered was that if one wore bright lipstick, then the eyes should be 'muted' and vice versa. Katrine supplied Lilou with creams and lotions for the trip to France, and then bags of gifts for Grand-mère Régine, Auntie Monique, and her cousin Aline, about whose existence Lilou had learned only a week prior.

The following morning, on the way to the airport, the Kellehers drove in silence. Lilou sat in the back of the car, battling exhaustion. She had not slept the previous night, anxious about the trip. Every time she thought of her mother's warnings about Grand-mère Régine, Lilou felt a knot form in her stomach. And then there was the advice about using make-up, the tiny jars in her suitcase, and the fact that right before they left the house, Katrine pulled her aside and applied eye cream, toner, a lotion, and eyeliner. Lilou stared at the reflection in the mirror and could barely recognize herself.

Am I better than Sammy? If Gary saw me now, would he like me? Lilou wondered. She liked how the eyeliner made her eyes seem big and mysterious. Her cheekbones seemed more prominent and that pleased her, too. *But all this doesn't matter. It's too late,* Lilou thought ruefully.

As they neared the airport, Lilou noticed her father looking at her in the rear-view mirror and frowning. Lilou averted her gaze and stared out the window. After they parked, both of her parents accompanied Lilou to the gate.

Her father walked up next to her. "Lilou, princess,

please, don't forget. You'll have a great time." His words seemed distant and strange.

"Yes, Daddy."

"Promise me you'll forget all about Pittsburgh and enjoy France, princess."

"Okay, Daddy." Lilou rubbed her temples, suddenly feeling like she was about to collapse. "Daddy, I need to use the bathroom," Lilou mumbled. As she walked off, she overheard her father's concerned voice:

"Katrine, what's happening? She can't go like this!"

And her mother's muffled response: "It was your idea!"

Chapter 8

GRAND-MÈRE

Lilou barely remembered the flight to Paris. She tried to sleep, but as soon as she closed her eyes, she saw Gary's face. Only it wasn't the same Gary from her dreams. The new version mocked her. Not the kind and considerate neighbor, the love of her life, her future husband, but a monster with sharp teeth and claws. He wasn't alone. A smaller, but a very similar, monster appeared beside him. It was Sammy. Rather than the ponytail, she had horns on her head, and hands equipped with sharp claws, like a tiger. The two of them laughed and mocked Lilou, and then produced a paper, holding it in their clawed paws. It was a wedding invitation. "Come and join us, Lilou," they said in unison and guffawed.

The smaller monster wrapped itself in a veil. Only the horns on top of its head tore through the muslin. Noticing the tear, the monster roared, showing its fangs, and yelled obscenities at Lilou, calling her names and blaming her for the ruined veil. It reached its claws to grab. Lilou screamed, pushed Sammy-the-monster out of the way, and immediately woke up.

Leaning against the window, Lilou clutched the thin airplane blanket for safety. *I am not going to make it*, a frightening thought flashed through her mind. Longing tugged at her for the safety of her bedroom, her bed, the familiar walls of her home. She spoke to no one on the flight, drank the water that the stewardess gave her in one gulp, but did not eat, staring at the tray in front of her blankly until it was taken away. Life had no meaning. Her mother's sudden interest, the make-up, the reassuring words from her father, all of that was useless, as Lilou stared into the abyss of life without Gary.

She wished for the plane to crash into the ocean. *That will be quick and easy, and I won't feel a thing*, she contemplated, as she noticed the white, fluffy clouds underneath. Noticing a small girl walking down the aisle with her mother, Lilou smiled at them and felt guilty at having those thoughts. Meanwhile, the plane steadily continued its journey and the quiet murmur of the engine indicated a smooth flight. Despair filled her mind as she tried to find an escape from a life without Gary. *He chose someone else. I am a total nobody, worthless. No one loves me*, Lilou agonized, as she looked out the window.

Occupied by grim thoughts, she had not even for a second considered what would happen after the flight, whether she would find her grandparents in the crowd, how they would even recognize each other, or how she would get around Paris once she landed. When it was time to disembark, Lilou did so reluctantly. She walked off the plane and froze, not sure what to do next. A man in a business suit bumped into her, grumbled and walked off without an apology. The incident forced her to move, and she followed the crowd to passport control. Once she'd managed that, she collected her luggage. Moving through the airport in a daze, she followed the other passengers.

Thinking of how long it would take to exchange her ticket to return home, she froze in place. That's when she noticed a small old woman in a black trench coat. The woman's head was covered with a light scarf, and she was gesticulating as she made her way towards Lilou. Before Lilou could understand what was happening, the woman yelped: "Ma petite!" and threw herself on Lilou, hugging her with bony arms. "My granddaughter! I've been waiting to meet you for over twenty years! Let me take a look at you!" The woman stepped back, gave Lilou a quick glance over, smiled, kissed her three times on the cheek as was customary in France, then hugged her again.

"Bonjour, Grand-mère," Lilou said uncertainly, feeling her cheeks turn beet red. In response, her grandmother's eyes filled with tears and she hugged even tighter.

"My sweet girl! You must be exhausted. Let's get your things and get you home. You need to relax!" The tiny old woman grabbed Lilou under the elbow and dragged her towards the exit.

Lilou followed, despite wanting only one thing – to run back on the plane and disappear forever. Her grandmother maneuvered aptly through the crowd, and Lilou walked behind, feeling as if she were floating. Wearing elegant heels and stockings with tiny arrows, Grand-mère's legs looked like those of a much younger woman.

That's where Maman learned her style, Lilou gathered and immediately felt sad that she had not inherited any of that elegance. *I am truly a gray mouse. No one will ever love me.* Lilou remembered the horned Sammy from her nightmares on the plane, and, despite herself, smiled at the torn veil of her nemesis. Revenge, even imaginary, felt sweet.

Régine stopped suddenly, and Lilou almost bumped into the old woman. They were out of the airport building and the grandmother whirled her head around, scanning her surroundings.

"Guillaume should be here somewhere," Régine noted absentmindedly. "It's so easy to get lost here! It's maddening, just impossible for a normal person to get their bearings. As if the airport had been built by a madman!" The old woman giggled. She craned her neck, trying to see, and reminded Lilou of a flamingo, so thin were her legs and so long her neck.

"A! Voilà! I see him!" Régine pointed to a beige car moving slowly in their direction.

The car stopped right in front of them, and, when the driver's door opened, Lilou saw a tall man wearing a fedora. His appearance left no doubt in her mind that they were related – his face was a replica of her mother's. The same pointed nose, bright eyes, and even the texture of the gray hair sticking out from under the hat looked exactly like her mother's blonde curls. Lilou froze in amazement as she stared at the man.

Seeing Lilou's reaction, her grandmother let out a giggle. "Lilou, chérie, don't be afraid. They do look alike, and there is an explanation for that!" Régine leaned into Lilou and whispered conspiratorially right into her ear. Lilou tried hard to understand her grandmother's rapid French, which was so unlike the everyday French speech she'd learned from her mother.

"You see, chouchou, your mother was conceived before marriage," Régine laughed, "we just couldn't control our passion, of course, but our little Katrine made sure your grand-père had no doubt as to his paternity. The second she was born, he was sure it was his progeny and, of course, we got married. Et voilà, now, forty-five years later, here we are!" Grandmother Régine adjusted her headscarf and coquettishly produced lipstick from her purse. She applied it with care, checking herself in a tiny pocket mirror.

Lilou's grandfather grunted as he waited. The second her grandmother put away her lipstick, he opened the trunk and, without saying a word, put Lilou's suitcase there. Lilou knew the suitcase was heavy – her mother had crammed it with Mary Kay cosmetics, but her grandfather lifted it with ease. Then he opened the passenger door for his wife, who fluttered into the seat, and, with a nod, opened the back door for Lilou.

"Hope your flight went well," the old man said. His voice was gruff and low. He twirled his mustache and reminded Lilou of Captain Haddock from the Tintin comics her mother adored and her father disliked. Lilou nodded and got into the car. The motor rumbled and they took off.

Within minutes, they were riding through the country-side. Lilou stared out the window, mesmerized. This was not at all the France that she'd imagined – no Eiffel Tower, no Louvre. Instead, she saw a forest, fields, winding roads. She'd never imagined France beyond images of Paris and did not know what to expect. The only thing she'd learned from her mother was that France was the standard of perfection, and that everything was better here. The food tasted better, the women dressed better, the houses were cozier. But what that perfection was like in reality, Lilou never imagined. Now, in the company of her grandparents, she found that France looked nice, but was not anything special.

Suddenly, Lilou remembered her mother's warnings about being careful with Grand-mère Régine. The old woman sitting in front appeared completely harmless. *I really don't know what Maman was talking about,* Lilou thought and sighed.

As if reading her mind, Régine said, "I am so glad that Katrine finally let you come and see us!" She rolled down the window and the wind ruffled Lilou's hair. "I just love the fresh air!" Lilou could barely hear her grandmother's words, but she nodded, showing agreement. "I so wish Marianne could also come and see us! How is she doing?" Régine turned back. Lilou froze, not sure how to respond. *Doesn't she know about the commune? About California?* She opened her mouth to speak, but her grandmother continued: "I guess she can't leave California for now. Well, that poor girl, I so wish things work out for her." *I guess Mother talks to Grand-mère? What does grandmother know about me?* Lilou stayed silent while her grandfather grunted in response.

"Of course, since this is your first time here, everything is new. You'll see our little town. Roissy. We live in a magical place, we really do," Grand-mère chuckled, "but pretty soon our idyll will be disrupted, they are about to open an airport right under our noses. Life will change. I hear it's supposed to be the biggest airport in the world. Of course, I should have known, a place like Roissy. It's a portal, such powerful energy." Régine shook her head. "And you'll see, we have everything one would need: the woods, a castle, nature, all in one place. Spectacular. Once you relax a little, we'll go to the woods, explore the forest."

"The forest?" Lilou opened her eyes wide in astonishment. *Why would I want to see the forest?*

"Yes, of course, the forest is amazing. Ours is small, but a great place to recharge!" Grand-mère noted with a smile while her husband hummed in response. "Guillaume doesn't approve of my hobbies," Régine laughed. "But at least he doesn't prevent me from visiting the forest and going there alone. I get up early every morning and head for the woods. Doesn't matter what the weather is like. Every day! I've been doing this for the last forty years, so he is used to it by now." Régine touched her husband's shoulder. "I don't know whether Katrine mentioned, I collect herbs for my healing work."

"No," Lilou responded. She felt the tips of her fingers grow cold. *What do I say? What kind of healing is she talking about? Maybe I didn't understand what she was saying.* Thoughts whirred in her mind.

"I am a healer. Natural healing, herbs, potions, various salves. I help people." The old woman turned to Lilou annunciating carefully, as if she had been reading Lilou's mind and knew exactly the doubts that were flashing through her granddaughter's mind about the ability to understand French.

"Your grandmother is a witch," Grandfather announced. Thinking his words a joke, Lilou chuckled, but her grandmother nodded in agreement.

"Yes, that's right. I am. I don't like to use that word to classify my profession, and of course, people are fearful once you tell them you are a witch. My goal is to help people, not frighten them. I am a good witch," Grandmother Régine's eyes sparkled. "You don't have to be afraid of me." The old woman winked at her granddaughter and turned to look at the road ahead.

Lilou's mouth gaped open. *This must be the reason why we never went to see Grand-mère. And that's why Maman never wanted me to meet my grandparents. But how is that possible? Witches don't exist in real life!*

"Are you feeling okay? You seem a little pale." She heard her grandmother's voice. "You must be exhausted from the trip, such a long flight. I've never flown on an airplane, just, well, we can talk about that later, but I can imagine how tiring it must be."

"I am fine," Lilou responded, feeling nausea rise in her throat. She remembered she hadn't eaten in over twenty-four hours and all of a sudden, a sharp, wild hunger overtook all of her senses. Her stomach rumbled.

"Guillaume, chéri, hurry, Lilou looks very pale," Lilou heard her grandmother's concerned tone, and her grandfather responded:

"Yes, I can see that." He pressed on the gas and the next thing she knew, Lilou was asleep.

She was in a deep, lush forest with emerald trees. From under the trees, tiny, adorable dwarfs appeared. They called Lilou to follow them. She spun around in a dance. Dressed in a flowing dress, she followed the dwarves to their dwelling. It was a dugout under one of the trees – a large oak with enormous roots bulging above ground. The dugout seemed too small for Lilou, but before she could tell the dwarves that she wouldn't fit into it, she was already inside. In the center sat a large wooden table with eight chairs around it. The space felt cozy and peaceful. There was a fire burning, warming up the room. The dwarves sat Lilou at the head of the table and then squeezed, three to the side, while the largest dwarf sitting directly across from Lilou. All wearing adorable hats, and, when they nodded, the hats shook in unison, as if to a beat.

"Here you are! We've been expecting you. And I must say, we were getting quite impatient!" one of tiny creatures said solemnly. Lilou looked at him in surprise. Unsure how to respond, she scanned the faces of the others for a hint. She did not feel like speaking, and continued to sit in silence. Lilou felt comfortable in their company and decided that she wouldn't mind staying there for some time. Suddenly, one of the dwarves stretched out his hand and started rubbing Lilou's arm. She brushed it away, but the dwarf said:

"Chérie, we're here." Lilou jerked awake and opened her eyes.

Their car had stopped in front of a two-story house. It looked so inviting that Lilou immediately liked it. A lush garden with roses blooming surrounded the house. The rose bushes were dense and appeared as if they were an extension of the home. Lilou nearly expected them to continue growing inside.Grandmother Régine hopped out of the car and ran to one of the bushes. She stroked the rosebud, mumbling softly, "Come here, my little one, please, please don't give up." Lilou noticed that the rose's leaves had a dryer appearance.

"Régine, please." Lilou heard her grandfather's voice. He was carrying her suitcase into the house. Lilou was the last one out of the car. She felt dizzy and wanted to lie down as quickly as possible. The strong pangs of hunger returned, and she felt like collapsing right there and then, amidst the rose bushes.

"Régine!" Lilou heard her grandfather's booming voice and then saw him walk over to his wife, who was still petting the rose bush.

"Oh, désolée, chérie[1]." Her grandmother rushed over to her granddaughter, grabbing Lilou by the elbow.

"Let's go, let's go, ma chouchou, I am so sorry, I've been trying to revive this bush for a few weeks, but it tells me it's very unhappy. I just don't understand why, it makes me wonder. So sad, because it used to be my favorite, and I thought we had a special relationship." Grand-mère sighed as she led Lilou inside the house. "Of course, you need to rest and to eat. I know in youth everything is different, desires are stronger, everything feels more powerful that it is. And then our senses dull, ah, just a part of life!"

The woman sighed. "The only thing that doesn't change is love! In old age, and I can tell you this, my dear child, love remains. We all want love and we all need it." Grand-mère gave Lilou a pointed look, and Lilou averted her eyes in embarrassment. *Does she know about Gary? Can she tell I am upset over a man? I don't need love,* Lilou thought bitterly.

"But I digress. Let me feed you, chérie. And then you need to sleep. Have you been having trouble sleeping?"

"Yes." Lilou nodded, unsure why she had admitted to having problems to her grandmother, whom she barely knew.

"Alright, alright, I can help you with those troubles," Régine mumbled under her nose, so softly that Lilou wasn't sure whether she heard the words correctly. *How does she know? Did Mother tell her about my problems?* Lilou wondered as she stepped inside of her grandparents' home. It was a small, cozy space. The smell inside a mix of rose and lavender, as if, just like Lilou suspected outside, the home was an extension of the garden.

"Please, make yourself comfortable." Régine pointed to a bedroom, and Lilou noticed her suitcase was already in there.

"Grand-mère…" Lilou started. Addressing a near stranger in this familiar way felt foreign, but Lilou forced herself to continue.

"Oui, chérie." Régine looked at Lilou with such tenderness that all of the girl's anxiety vanished in an instant.

"Maman gave me some cosmetics, lotions, Mary Kay. Maybe you've heard of it? They are very good, excellent quality, and, I think you'll like it." Lilou tried to speak of Mary Kay with as much esteem as she'd heard her mother do, but found her speech, once translated into French, lacking. There wasn't a hint of her mother's excitement in her voice, no promise of the magical powers of Mary Kay, ready to transform customers into amazing beauties.

"Oh, of course, of course. You can show me later."

Régine smiled, and waved her hand dismissively. "But right now, why don't you freshen up and then we'll eat?"

"Okay." Lilou stepped into the bedroom, leaving her grandmother at the threshold.

"Oh! I almost forgot, I think I need to give you some valerian, it's a great sedative, you need to balance a few things out. I also have some great Chinese herbs I found recently, and I know now that they were meant for you! Just perfect for you, Lilou. A wonderful sedative, and you'll sleep very well!" Without waiting for an answer, her grandmother rushed into the kitchen with the agility of a much younger woman. A few seconds later, Lilou heard the sound of pouring water and clanking pots.

She looked around her bedroom. There was a neatly made bed in the center of the room decorated with a tyrian purple bed spread. Curtains with a floral pattern of a nondescript hue, a mix of lavender and mulberry, hung on the windows. On the bedside table, she found a book called *An Herbalist's Guide to French Forests*, and a Paris guidebook. Lilou grabbed the guidebook and started flipping through the pages. But a moment later, the intense, all-encompassing hunger returned. Her hands trembling, Lilou opened the suitcase, unpacked boxes of cosmetics to present to her grandmother, and headed for the kitchen.

The table was set for three. Régine stood next to the stove, stirring what seemed like an army of pots and pans. Lilou's grandfather appeared in the kitchen and gave his wife an approving look as he sat down at the table.

"It's all ready, chéri," Régine noted and pecked her husband on the cheek.

Lilou looked at the dishes on the table. There was a salad, bread, chicken, potatoes. The food was simple, but gave a festive and inviting appearance. Lilou had heard from her mother that in France, the afternoon meal was an important one. But all that was theoretical knowledge. In the Kelleher household, the main meal was dinner, served at 7pm by her Americanized mother. Dinner time did not change, scheduled for when her father arrived at home from work. Lilou's mother, despite grumbling about the 'lack of real food' in America, cooked mostly American dishes, and Lilou did not understand what the reference meant until she sat at the table with her grandparents.

Everything looked brighter, fresher, and tastier. The tomatoes in the salad were crimson red and smelled delicious. The lettuce was green, bursting with flavor. And the grilled chicken that her grandmother produced from the oven begged to be eaten. Lilou, already ravenously hungry, could barely control herself so as not to wolf down her meal.

"This is delicious!" She couldn't help herself, taking a bite of the chicken.

"Ha! Your grandmother isn't only great at potions, as you can see," her grandfather joked.

"Good that you reminded me. Speaking of potions! I nearly forgot." Régine rushed to the stove and Lilou noticed a small red pot with steam rising. Lilou froze. *So they were serious? She is really a witch?* The frightening thought flashed through her mind.

"This is an infusion I made just for you." Grand-mère stirred the contents of the pot, moving her hands over the steam, then smelled the steam rising from it. She turned off the stove and poured the contents of the pot on a strainer. She handed Lilou a full cup of the liquid. "Drink this. It will make you feel much, much better."

Lilou smelled the drink and balked. It was acrid.

"You must drink it quickly, don't think about it!" The old woman commanded, and her voice sounded so stern that Lilou did not dare contradict her. On her second taste, she found that the mixture tasted pleasant despite a slight bitterness. She finished the cup.

"Good, very good," her grandmother nodded in approval. "And now, off to bed! You need to rest!"

"Thank you," Lilou responded. Her limbs grew heavy, and she felt as if her eyelids were about to close on their own accord. She excused herself and went to her bedroom. Once there, she collapsed on the bed, drew the soft blanket over her head, and fell into a deep sleep.

Chapter 9
THE DREAM

She dreamed. In her dream, Lilou found herself once more in a magical forest. Back with the tiny dwarves, sitting in their abode, at the helm of an oak table. This time, she paid more attention to the room. The walls looked as if they had been carved of stone. *Strange, with the space being under a tree,* Lilou thought. The fire still burned, and she felt warm and cozy. Suddenly, Lilou remembered the dwarves had complained to her and were expecting an answer. She felt her cheeks grow red in embarrassment from not knowing what to say.

"We've waited for a long time for you, Lilou!" As if on cue, the head dwarf said, continuing their earlier conversation. His face looked familiar, and she tried to place him. *Maybe he is from the cartoon? Where could I have seen him?* Lilou scrambled to understand her connection to the little man, but in vain.

"What do you mean?" She tried to stay calm and pleasant.

"You are special. You have powers. Witch powers."

"What?" Even in her dream, she felt her mouth gape open in a gasp.

"Oh, yes, Lilou, you need to embrace your powers!" The lead dwarf smiled and rubbed his head. He was wearing a cap, like a train conductor, and pants with suspenders.

"But I am just a girl!" Lilou yelled, forgetting her prior efforts to be pleasant and polite.

"Yes, you are a girl, but a special one! You have great powers, Lilou!" the lead dwarf said.

"But who are you? How do you know me?"

"We are magical creatures, guardians of nature. We speak to the forest and the stones. We navigate the space where time stands still." The expression on his face dignified.

"Time stands still? What does that mean?" Lilou shook her head.

"You will find out in due course." The dwarves nodded in unison, seven heads bobbing at the same time. It was a comical scene, only Lilou could not laugh.

"But I am no witch! I am studying. I'll be an accountant."

In response, the lead dwarf giggled, and then the other six tiny men also laughed. They bent over in laughter, and the entire room was filled with the sound of their merriment.

"Please, this isn't fair. Why are you laughing at me?" Lilou protested.

"It's just that the profession you chose for yourself couldn't be more removed from your true calling!" The lead dwarf shook his head. "How funny life is, really, but you will learn, you will find out!" He raised his tiny hand to the ceiling, as if pointing to the sky.

"I don't understand! It's my passion. Math. I love

accounting. I've worked very hard, and I am good at it!" Lilou said with conviction, forgetting all about her disastrous end of the last semester.

"Of course, Lilou, of course. Your life probably seems very straightforward to you right now, but you will remember us in the future. We'll come to you again when you are ready. We are there to help you. We'll guide you to your true calling." The main dwarf was no longer laughing, but an encouraging smile appeared on his face.

"Thank you, I guess!" Lilou rolled her eyes.

She knew she was being rude, but she did not like what the dwarves were telling her. The room felt claustrophobic. She wanted to leave the tiny creatures and to return to the lush forest, to the beautiful field where she danced in the beginning of the dream. *I've had this dream before.* The thought flashed through her mind. The forest and the tiny men, she remembered that she'd had this conversation with them before. Many conversations. She'd been in that room and she'd met the dwarves hundreds of times. Only each time she forgot about the dream the moment it was over.

The next moment she saw that the face of the tiny man was not the face of a dwarf, but that of a wolf. Instead of hands, she saw the long wolf's claws. The wolf-dwarf smiled at her.

"Wolfgang!" Lilou gasped, as she remembered the name of her favorite toy as a child. "I'm sorry, I am so sorry I forgot about you." She felt tears well up in her eyes. The wolf extended its paw, and, to her surprise, she shook it. The wolf's paw felt warm and pleasant to the touch.

The next thing she knew, Lilou was sitting up in bed, staring at the unfamiliar wall. For one brief moment, she thought she was in her bedroom in Pittsburgh, and was startled to see that the room looked completely different.

And then Lilou remembered she was in France, at her grandparents' house in Roissy.

The wolf! she thought and wiped beads of sweat from her forehead. *But I must get up, it's probably late, what am I even doing?* Lilou forced herself to get out of bed. She hobbled to the kitchen, feeling drowsy.

"How was your nap?" her grandmother asked, giving an assessing look. Lilou felt her legs wobble, as she leaned on the kitchen table.

"It was nice, thank you," Lilou croaked. Her throat was parched, but she was too embarrassed to ask her grandmother for something to drink.

"Have a seat, relax, I hear life in America is always so rushed." Her grandmother gave her a bright smile. "Here, we don't like to rush." Suddenly self-conscious, Lilou edged to the dinner table and slid into one of the chairs.

"So, this afternoon, we'll go to the forest! Why wait?" Régine shrugged. "I think it'll be a refreshing walk for you, and it's very nice to walk around after a long journey. To connect with Mother Earth."

Lilou nodded, while having an internal struggle. *Mother Earth? Why does my grandmother sound like a hippie?* Suddenly, she saw a vivid image of the wolf and remembered shaking its paw. *Oh, I am definitely losing my mind.* And then another thought occurred to her. *Maybe I am still asleep?* Lilou rubbed her eyes.

"If it weren't for the forest, we would have never survived the war." She heard Régine's voice.

"The war?" Lilou sat up straight.

"Oh, yes, the war was terrible. The Germans were everywhere, we had to hide in the forest. There is so much power there, and I knew every path, every little leaf of every tree. I knew how to get food, find shelter. I saved my girls. Your mother and your aunt. You'll go to see Monique in a couple of days." Her grandmother smiled and Lilou nodded in understanding. Her grandmother was speaking of practical information, finally something that Lilou could follow.

"Lilou, there is a lot more that I need to tell you," her grandmother said, in a severe tone.

"Okay." A feeling of panic overtook Lilou's whole being, and the tips of her fingers grew cold.

"No need to worry," Régine said, and Lilou swallowed hard. *Is she reading my mind?* flashed in Lilou's head. "In this world, everything happens for a reason. Everything unfolds in due course. I've looked at the cards, I know that it's not your time yet. We must wait. Do you understand?" Régine stared so intently that Lilou felt as if her grandmother could see right through her.

"I, I am sorry! I don't understand!" Lilou now felt her cheeks grow flushed with embarrassment. "Wait for what?"

"Oh, my poor dear, didn't your mother ever tell you? But that's just criminal!" Régine shook her head indignantly.

"Tell me what? Maman rarely talks to me at all!" Lilou spewed out and suddenly started crying. All the years of suppressing the need for her mother's love, the constant feeling of rejection overpowered her.

"Ma chérie. Ma petite chérie." Régine walked over to Lilou and gave her a kiss on the forehead. "You are such a lovely girl! I could not have imagined a better successor! I am so thrilled that we met! At last!"

"Successor?" Lilou's mouth gaped open and her tears dried up.

"Of course. Successor in my line of business." Régine gave Lilou a firm stare.

"By your line of business, you mean," Lilou cleared her throat, "witchcraft?" She expected her grandmother to protest, to laugh, to tell her she had a vivid imagination, but Régine nodded vigorously and announced:

"Yes! Exactement[1]! You are my successor, Lilou!" The old woman clapped her hands.

"I am not a witch!" Lilou protested, no longer trying to sound polite.

"Not yet, because you are too young. To become a practicing witch of our caliber, you have to have children of your own. That's key."

I'll never have children of my own, now that Gary is getting married to someone else, Lilou thought, relief flooding her body. She slumped on the chair.

"I've been expecting you to come into this world, Lilou." Her grandmother sat next to her and took her hands. For a second, Lilou remembered the wolf's paw and, holding her grandmother's hand, she felt the same softness. "The day after your mother got pregnant with you, I had a dream. Mind you, she didn't even know she was pregnant! I called Katrine and told her she would soon give birth to the most powerful witch of our family line yet."

"That's some kind of mistake." Lilou shook her head in disbelief.

"I don't make mistakes, Lilou. I've been practicing for over forty years. And before me, my mother, and grand-mother, and so on."

"Why me?"

"Because I can pass my gift to one descendant, a girl!" Grandmother Régine's face took on a somber expression. "If I don't do it before I die, my powers will be lost and will haunt me in the afterlife. A witch must find a successor. In our family tradition, the witch powers are passed on to the oldest daughter. But your mother wanted nothing to do with my line of business. Then your auntie Monique decided the same. Neither one of them had much of a gift anyway, so I decided to wait for a granddaughter. And I have the three: you, Marianne, and Aline. Out of the three, you are the only one who has the gift."

Lilou's mouth gaped open, as she listened to her grandmother.

"You know what? Let's go for a walk, and I'll tell you the rest!" Grandmother Régine moved in the direction of the front door, Lilou followed until they were in a beautiful forest.

Her grandmother reminded Lilou of a young girl, as she skipped down the path and showed her the gifts of the forest. Lilou followed along, awestruck.

"I want to show you some herbs, so you can learn the basics now," her grandmother said

Strangely, Lilou felt an incredible lightness, a connectedness, to Régine. It was a feeling she'd never experienced with her mother. The worry about Gary and Sammy receded to the background, and not once during their walk did Lilou think about her lost love or rival.

"Grandmother, why did you bring food with us? Are we going to eat here?" Lilou asked, noticing a bag of bread that magically materialized in her grandmother's hands.

"Oh, that's for the guardians of the forest." Her grandmother let out a laugh. "They like treats." Régine stopped and looked around. "Actually, we can feed them right here! You must have sensed their presence."

"No, it's just a coincidence!" Lilou protested. "I only noticed the bag just now."

"No, no, dear girl, embrace your powers. You are connected to the forest creatures, just like I am. Let's feed our forest friends. This is the perfect spot!" Régine pointed to a stump. "Right here!"

Lilou stood still, staring at her grandmother, while

Régine handed over the bag with dried bread. The next moment, Lilou reached inside the bag, as if she'd done this very thing thousands of time before. Just like her grandmother said, Lilou felt connected to the forest, to the creatures around her. A feeling of beautiful, all-encompassing love for the world around her came over Lilou. She whispered, "Enjoy the treats, little guys," as she placed the bread on the tree stump. She heard the leaves of a tree above her rustle. Then, the drum of a woodpecker.

"They heard you! Just perfect!" Régine clapped her hands. "It all confirms that I am right. There are different kinds of witches out there. And our kind, we are the nature witches. We give voice to those around us that don't speak in a conventional way. From stones and trees to the little creatures. Elves, home protectors, gnomes, fairies!"

"You speak to them?" Lilou scanned her grandmother's face, her head spinning from the information her grandmother had just shared.

"They speak to me! I just translate it for those who care to listen."

"I don't understand."

"It's very simple, Lilou. Remember the fairy tales you read as a child? All those little creatures? Well, they exist in real life. In the olden days, people knew how to connect with them. If you wanted to build a house, you didn't just start building it. You asked for permission from the creatures who were living on that land. Or you came to someone like me to help you communicate with the creatures. Now people refuse to hear them, try to ignore them, forgetting that elves and gnomes can be very helpful. Or quite disruptive, if you offend them!"

Lilou heard a soft rustling. She expected to see a squirrel or a chipmunk, but instead, she saw a wolf. He scowled at her.

"Time to wake up, Lilou," the wolf said. "You've been sleeping for a long time. It's time to explore Paris with your grandmother."

"But I am awake!" Lilou protested. She looked around the forest, but the lush greenery disappeared. "I was just giving bread to the forest creatures, I was just…" Lilou sat up in bed. Back her grandmother's house, in the bedroom. *Have I been asleep this whole time? Did I dream it all? But it was so real!*

Her grandmother stood on the threshold. "Time to wake up, Lilou."

Lilou balked. *Is she the wolf?*

"How was your night?"

"Night? I thought I was just taking a nap," Lilou responded.

"We let you sleep through the night. You must have been exhausted." Régine smiled. "Let's have some breakfast and head out into the city. Grand-père will take us!"

Lilou rubbed her eyes. The memory of her dream disappeared in a flash. *I am going to Paris!* Lilou grabbed the guidebook from the bedside table and followed her grandmother to the kitchen.

Chapter 10
LYON

Right after breakfast, they drove into the city. Lilou clutched the Paris guidebook in her hands, tracing their journey on a small map in the back. At first, as they left Roissy, she didn't find the scenery particularly special and even felt disappointed, looking at the roads and small cottages and fields that peppered the hills. But quickly the countryside turned into the suburbs and suddenly, they were driving on Boulevard Beaumarchais. The avenue was shaded, with beautiful buildings on each side, each one a masterpiece.

It's beautiful! So this is what Maman meant about France being special. Lilou suddenly understood. The city took her breath away. She forgot all about the guidebook and stared, her mouth gaping open. The passersby going through their morning chores appeared magnificent and mysterious. *I wish I could live here!* she thought. The car turned and suddenly she saw the Seine. The river glistened in the sun and looked magical, its banks clad in beautiful brick, so unlike the barren banks of the three rivers Lilou had seen all her life in Pittsburgh.

"Wow!" Lilou gasped, only then realizing she said it out loud.

"It's gorgeous, isn't it!" Régine turned to face her, a kind smile on her face. "And this is just the beginning!"

Her grandparents first took her to see Notre Dame de Paris. Lilou thought she knew what to expect and considered herself an expert in Gothic architecture, after having several classes each semester at the Cathedral of Learning in Oakland. But the delicate beauty of Notre Dame, the intricate stone carvings, the endless flying buttresses, made its Pittsburgh counterpart pale in comparison.

"How did they do this?" Lilou asked her grandmother, when they stood outside of the building, staring at the rose window in the center of the façade.

"Lots of hard work and a little bit of magic, chou-chou," her grandmother smiled at her.

In the hopes of remembering as much as possible about Notre Dame, Lilou bought several postcards with different views of the cathedral.

'Grand-mère, I am thinking of sending this one to my parents." she said, as she flipped through the postcards and stopped at the one with the view of the side of the cathedral, with the pretty garden of the Square Jean XXIII. "And I can tell them we are sitting on a bench right here as I write to them!" Lilou gave her grandmother a broad smile.

"That's a great choice," Régine gave her a nod of approval. "Wonderful idea."

The city was limitless, and Lilou fell in love with every part of it. Her grandparents took her to see museums, gardens, the Eiffel Tower. Lilou memorized the guide-book. Paris! She got to visit beautiful Paris. She only thought of Gary once, when she saw a couple kissing. Then, tears welled up in her eyes, but Lilou brushed the thought of her neighbor away, and returned to enjoying the city.

A week later, Lilou sat on her bed, staring at her closed suitcase. *I can't believe it's been a week!* she thought, flipping the Paris guidebook in her hands.

"Lilou, time to go," her grandmother called.

A second later, her grandfather appeared in the doorway. "Are you ready?" He grunted and reached for the suitcase.

"Yes," Lilou nodded and got up. She averted her eyes, as she followed her grandfather to the car.

They drove to Paris for a different reason: so Lilou could take the train from Gare de Lyon to see her aunt in Lyon. *Goodbye, Paris,* she thought, as they approached the station. Her grandfather got her suitcase out of the trunk, and they walked to the train in a solemn procession. She heard the train announcement and her heart sank. She did not want to leave her grandparents.

Why do I have to go see this aunt? she thought.

The only consolation was that the visit to Lyon was only for one week, and then she would be back to stay with her grandparents before leaving for Pittsburgh.

"See you soon! Bisous!" Her grandmother kissed her on the forehead and gave her a tight squeeze. *I don't know why Maman warned me about Grand-mère,* Lilou thought, as she got on the train and walked down the aisle, looking for her seat. *She is harmless.*

Lilou made herself comfortable and examined the basket of food that her grandmother prepared for her. The train jerked and started moving, while Lilou glued her face to the window. They were gathering speed, and the Parisian scenery soon gave way to the countryside. Instead of apartment buildings and city blocks, she saw trees, fields, and winding roads. Suddenly, Lilou noticed a gray silhouette running alongside the train.

The wolf!

She could see him following the train, his gray fur glistening in the sun. The memory of the wolf she saw in her dream came back to her. *Can wolves run that fast?* The next second, the creature looked directly at her and Lilou gasped.

She heard the conductor's voice: "Ticket, please". The conductor's cap looked exactly like the one she'd seen the lead dwarf wearing, and Lilou gulped. She tried to remember the conversation with the dwarves and what they told her about her profession, but the conductor stared at her. Lilou reached into her bag, fumbling for the ticket. The conductor punched it then moved on, and Lilou forgot about the dream the second the conductor disappeared from view. She reached for the basket. As she bit into her sandwich, a strange thought occurred to her.

I am just like Little Red Riding Hood. The wolf, the forest, the grandmother, the basket of food. Lilou chuckled.

She must have drifted off to sleep, because before she knew it, the train had arrived in Lyon. Lilou grabbed her suitcase and climbed down on to the platform. Right away, she saw a woman waving at her. Two children, a reed-thin boy of about ten and a girl of about sixteen, stood slightly behind their mother. After hesitating for a moment, Lilou waved back.

That must be Monique and Aline, Lilou thought of the girl, who looked exactly like their aunt, and had the same bright blue, bulging eyes. *And I guess there is a boy, too.*

"Lilou! Bienvenue à Lyon[1]!" Auntie Monique yelped and kissed Lilou on the cheek. Lilou noticed tears in her aunt's eyes. "I can't believe this is the first time we see each other in person! You look just like your father!"

"I do." Lilou nodded. This was not a compliment, but she decided not to get upset at her aunt.

"I miss Katrine so much! I wish she'd come to France and visit us here someday. Please tell your mother we are all waiting for her! This is Aline, my oldest." Monique nudged the girl forward, and then, nodding in the direction of the boy. "And Ambroise." Aline sniggered, and the boy turned red.

"Nice to meet you all," Lilou nodded vigorously. *Why didn't anyone mention this boy to me?* Lilou wondered.

"So we are going to head back to our place. You must be tired. You need to get some rest!" Lilou gulped under her aunt's assessing stare. *She probably thinks I am ugly,* Lilou decided. The woman made her feel self-conscious, the feeling remarkably similar to how Lilou felt around her mother.

"En voiture, Simone[2]." Auntie Monique smiled as they walked up to a parked car.

Lilou half-expected a chauffeur to appear, but her aunt opened the driver's side and sat confidently behind the wheel. "Aline and Ambroise will ride in the back." She smiled and invited Lilou to the passenger's seat next to her.

"Who is Simone?" Lilou stared at her aunt in surprise. In response, Auntie Monique giggled and shook her head.

"Oh, it's an expression. Didn't Katrine teach you?"

"No." Lilou turned red in embarrassment.

"But your French is so good!" Auntie Monique gave Lilou a quizzical stare. "Your Maman and I, we loved Simone des Forest when we were little. She was a French female race car driver in the 1930s, amazing woman! World famous. Aline knows all about her, a great role model." Monique looked over at her daughter, who nodded in agreement.

"I see." Lilou shifted her eyes, feeling inadequate. She

felt her hands get clammy in discomfort and badly wanted to return to her grandmother's place. *Why did I even come here? I am going to hate it in Lyon.*

"Our building is right next to the best place in Lyon! Parc de la tete d'Or!" Auntie Monique announced, as they were driving away from the train station. "We have two great rivers, the Rhone and the Saone!" Auntie Monique said proudly. "And even though I am not a native Lyonnaise, I love the city very much."

"I see." Lilou tried to give her voice a tone of excitement, ashamed that she had not taken the time to read about Lyon before coming to the city. She stared out the window and started to feel captivated by the city.

"I wanted to be close to nature. Ideally I would have loved to live in the country, but Claude, my husband, wanted to be in the city. So we found the perfect compromise. I go for a walk in the park every day. It's gorgeous. The roses there are just splendid. Do you like nature?" Auntie Monique looked over at Lilou, while gripping the steering wheel.

"Yes, I like nature." *Who would ever say that they don't like nature?* Lilou pondered.

A few minutes later, they parked in front of a white five-story apartment building. When they entered the lobby, Lilou noticed the railings: wrought-iron, with intricate designs. The ceiling was incredibly high, and Lilou had the impression of entering a palace.

"Wow!" Lilou exclaimed, and immediately put a hand to her mouth, embarrassed to have openly shared her admiration.

"It's beautiful, isn't it?" Monique winked at Lilou, eyes glistening with pleasure. "I had the same reaction the first time I visited this place." Her aunt pressed the elevator button.

When the elevator door opened, Lilou was surprised to see how small it was. It could only accommodate two people at a time if they were to take up Lilou's suitcase.

"Aline and Ambroise will wait," Monique stated, not leaving any room for hesitation, and Lilou suddenly found herself alone with her energetic aunt in the narrow space. The ride up in the elevator, which only took a minute, seemed like an eternity. Lilou felt as if she were under a microscope, with her aunt noticing all her flaws. From her overly long nose and mousy hair to the nondescript color of her eyes, that were neither brown nor gray, but some strange shade in-between.

They entered the apartment, Lilou dragging the suitcase behind her, badly wishing to return to her grandmother's cottage, which felt so much more like home. Lilou took in the apartment.

Posh. She thought, trying not to gape at the chandeliers, brass door handles in shapes of animal heads and antique furniture. Before Lilou could say anything, Aline and Ambroise entered the apartment.

"Aline, show Lilou to her room, please," Monique ordered and threw a stern look at her daughter.

The girl nodded and mumbled, "Oui, Maman[3]," then, winking at Lilou, led her down the long corridor. They found themselves in a small bedroom at the very end.

"This is where you'll sleep! This is actually my bedroom, but I moved out so you can stay here," Aline said with pride in her voice. "Do you like it? Maman has just remodeled."

"Yes," Lilou said uncertainly, taking in the narrow bed by the window and a small bedside table. The space looked spartan and uninviting, completely different from the rest of the apartment.

"Maman brought an interior designer. She thinks that

we need to keep up with the times. This style is minimalist, very modern, there is little furniture, just the bare essentials. We are trying out the dark green and brown in here and then Maman might change the rest of the apartment, too," Aline explained.

"I see." Lilou nodded. She was about to ask Aline why the color combination for a young girl's bedroom needed to be so somber, but Aline noted:

"You can put your suitcase right here." She pointed to a spot near the door.

"Thank you, and where will you sleep?" Lilou asked.

"Oh, I'll be sleeping in our guest bedroom. It used to be a governess's room. It's small. Maman told us that in America you are used to huge spaces, so you would expect a bigger room. Is that true?" Aline gave her an expectant look.

"I guess so." Lilou gulped. "I never thought about it. But I don't want you to have to switch rooms because of me." Lilou stared at her cousin, wide-eyed.

Aline shrugged and adjusted her curls. "It's really not a big deal, and besides, it's fun. I'll come visit you at night!"

"Great," Lilou said, not wanting to offend her cousin. The idea of spending time together with this near stranger at night made her uneasy. "I am just going to unpack."

Aline showed no intention of leaving. Lilou unzipped her suitcase, and Aline leaned over her, silently examining the contents of her bag. "My mother sent over cosmetics, Mary Kay. Maybe you heard of them? It's for Auntie Monique." Lilou felt the need to speak, anything to avoid an uncomfortable silence.

Ignoring the explanation, Aline plopped on the bed and gave Lilou a quizzical look. "Do you have a friend?"

"A… friend?" Lilou cleared her throat. She felt her whole face turn beet red in shame, remembering Gary. His betrayal, her tears and broken dreams. "I, I do have a friend," Lilou lied. "But we can't be together. There are, umm, certain issues," she added, suddenly emboldened. Lying about Gary was easy and familiar.

"Oh, why? Is it because you're in France now? You've broken up for the summer?" Aline jumped on the bed. Her eyes twinkled with excitement.

"Well, umm, yes," Lilou responded. Aline was right. She and Gary only broke up for the summer. The lies came more easily now. She pushed the idea of Sammy, of Gary's upcoming nuptials out of her mind and swallowed hard. "Gary is my boyfriend." Lilou scanned Aline's face for a reaction. Her cousin nodded in encouragement. "Gary loves me. He wanted me to stay home. Couldn't take the thought of being apart from me, but my parents made me go to France. Once I return, we'll be together!" Lilou could almost picture Gary's face and their tearful goodbye.

"That's so romantic!" Aline clapped and smiled widely.

Seeing her cousin's smile, Lilou knew at once. *Everything will work out.* Yes, my Gary is special." Lilou nodded, now fully enthralled in her lie.

"So, what's he like? Your beloved?"

"Beloved!" Lilou latched onto the word, savoring its sound. She stopped unpacking and sat on the bed next to her cousin. "He is handsome, tall, and strong. Has a nice, manly chin and blue eyes. Blonde, but he tans really well in the summer, and he is really smart, he's almost done with college." Describing Gary's looks that she'd studied in secret for so many years, Lilou got carried away by the fantasy.

"You are lucky! American men are incredibly hot! Do they all look like the Marlboro man from the billboards?"

"Well, I am not sure." Lilou giggled. "But now that you

mention it, my Gary does look like the Marlboro man. Except, he isn't a cowboy.

"I'll definitely come and visit you to meet all those hot guys!" Aline raised her voice.

"What guys?" Auntie Monique walked into the bedroom without knocking. "What's all this fracas?"

"Maman, we are just joking." Aline fidgeted on the bed.

"Don't be so loud, Aline." Monique looked at her daughter with disapproval. Lilou expected Aline to apologize, but her cousin shrugged in response. "Your father doesn't like the noise. And what's all this talk? You are only seventeen!"

"Okay, Maman." Aline rolled her eyes.

"We're about to sit down for lunch. Ten minutes. Lilou, how do you find your room? Did Aline show you everything?"

"Thank you, everything is perfect," Lilou nodded and looked at the floor, wanting to disappear. Gone was her carefree mood.

"Maman, we'll be right there," her cousin said, as Auntie Monique left the room. Lilou was about to get up, but the girl grabbed Lilou by the hand, as if they were co-conspirators. Leaning closely in, Aline whispered: "Don't mind Maman, she gets stressed out when we have visitors. Listen, do you know about our grandmother? Did you figure it out?"

"Figure out what?" Lilou felt her hands get clammy. A faint memory of the dream she'd had at her grandmother's flashed in her mind, but she pushed it away.

"Our grandmother is a witch!" Aline whispered these words right into her ear, and Lilou jerked. Her head started spinning. *Witch, witch, witch,* the French word 'sorcière' sounded like the toll of the bell.

"Witch?" Lilou repeated out loud and swallowed hard.

"Yes! She can do spells! She is a practicing witch! Very powerful!" Aline stared right at her, and the pupils of her cousin's eyes had dilated, making them look almost pitch-black.

Aline spoke fast and in French, but Lilou understood everything at once. Her grandmother's potion, the trips to the forest, the explanations that Grand-mère had given her. It all came together. In an instant, Lilou remembered the dream and knew it was real. She heard her grandmother's words clearly. *'I can only pass my gift to one descendant, a girl! If I don't do it before I die, my powers will be lost. You are my successor, Lilou'*.

"She even speaks to trees, animals, and herbs. Clients come to her for spells. All these women!" Aline whispered conspiratorially right into her ear. "I was at her place two years ago, and I saw everything. It was the middle of the night, but I woke up and I saw her do a reading. She laid these cards on the table and the woman sat across from her, crying. Her husband was cheating, but she wanted to know for sure, and grandmother told her everything. She could see it from the cards!"

"But how?" Lilou exclaimed despite herself. "That's impossible!"

"I am not sure. But Grand-mère even described the other woman, and the client immediately guessed who it was! I think our grandmother can do love spells too. I am not sure, but I researched this stuff. I found a book about witchcraft. I am going to be a witch, just like Grand-mère."

"What?" Lilou shrieked, and immediately put a hand over her mouth, remembering Monique's admonishment.

"I am going to inherit Grand-mère's special powers. I heard that she has to pass on her powers to someone. To a bloodline relative, a girl. And that's going to be me!" Aline smiled proudly.

"Does this mean our mothers are both witches?" Lilou opened her eyes wide.

"Oh, not at all! Actually, your mother and mine, they want nothing to do with witchcraft. That's why yours moved away, married an American. And that's why my mother lives in Lyon. They didn't want to be close to Grand-mère."

The rest of the dream came back to Lilou. *Your mother, Katrine, wanted nothing to do with my line of business.* Lilou stared at Aline, her mouth gaping open, remembering her mother's words about France. The curt words to describe Grand-mère, the distance between them, her warnings. It was as if pieces of a puzzle, once scattered and unnoticed, at last fit together and formed an explanation that Lilou did not know that she'd been seeking.

All this time, Maman was trying to protect me! Lilou understood and felt tears well up in her eyes. What she'd taken to be her mother's lack of love had been an expression of care. *Maman didn't want me to become a witch!*

"I overheard my mom one night on the telephone. She has this best friend. They tell each other everything." Aline rattled on, not paying any attention to Lilou. "And that's how I knew. Because my mom, she's like yours, she doesn't like witchcraft. So, Grand-mère cannot pass it on to either of them. And they made a pact, you know, our moms, to stop the bloodline. To do everything to avoid witchcraft in their lives. And so that's why they never told us about it. That's why Ambroise and I barely know her." Her cousin was speaking fast and suddenly stopped and stared at Lilou. "You got what I said, right?" Aline tilted her head.

In response, Lilou nodded and cleared her throat, her voice hoarse. "What do you mean by bloodline?"

"It's in our bloodline. Witchcraft. Our grand-mère got it from her mom, and so on. Twenty seven generations, until ours. That's what I heard."

"Twenty seven?" Lilou closed her eyes. "But that's centuries."

"I know! Isn't it amazing?" Aline pulled at Lilou's sleeve.

"It's a lot."

"That's why I am going to be *the one*!" Aline continued, now encouraged.

"How do you know?" Lilou frowned.

"I won't let twenty seven generations of witchcraft go to waste. I will inherit Grandmother's powers." Aline clapped her hands and smiled brightly. "I am going to show you tonight. I'll prove it. Grand-mère will transfer her powers to me once she is done practicing. And in the meantime, I am going to start on my own."

"Why?" Lilou swallowed. She wanted to escape, to get away from this strange girl, who no longer seemed like an innocent seventeen-year-old, but a frightening sorceress.

"I want to have clients, so that women will come to see me from all over France. I'll be famous!" Aline rubbed her hands.

At that moment, they heard Monique's booming voice. "Lunch is ready!"

Without another word, Lilou dashed to the dining room.

Chapter 11
THE LUNCH

The table was set for five, with a white table cloth, napkins, and a full china service. Each setting had several forks, knives, and spoons. A large soup dish adorned the middle of the table, and steam rose from it through the lid. Lilou hesitated. At home, they never sat down to eat formally, at least not since Marianne had run away.

Lilou heard the rustling of a newspaper and a cough. She nearly jumped in surprise and turned to see a short, balding man with a protruding belly. He rose from the armchair that stood obscured in the shadows in the corner of the room.

"Bonjour!" The man walked over to Lilou and extended his hand. "Have we met? Are you a friend of Aline's?" He stared at Lilou in confusion.

"Non, chéri, this is Lilou, your niece. Katrine's daughter," Auntie Monique appeared and said in a loud whisper.

"Katrine." The squat man squinted, as if trying to ascertain the identity of another unknown person.

"My sister. She lives in America." Monique sighed. "Remember?"

"Oh! Bien sûr, bien sûr[1]." The little man folded the newspaper and set it on the armchair. "Of course, I completely forgot. So busy with work these days, so busy, you must excuse me."

Frozen in place, Lilou felt unable to speak from the shock of meeting the head of the household, who did not have the faintest idea about her visit. *Did they not tell him I was coming?* she wondered. *This is too strange. It doesn't seem like he even wants to have me here.*

"Lilou, this is my husband, Claude." Monique smiled.

"Nice to meet you." Lilou squeezed out, feeling a knot form in her stomach.

"So, did you come all the way from America?" Claude asked, clearing his throat. Noticing that the rest of the family had assembled in the dining room, he said, "Let's sit down and eat." He pointed at the table.

"Yes." Lilou nodded eagerly, attempting to sound pleasant. She wished to disappear and to be alone, far away from this strange family.

"Claude is a little absent-minded," Auntie Monique said, shaking her head wearily. Her whole figure showed that her husband's character had caused her a great deal of trouble, but she bore it in stride.

"No problem," Lilou nodded. She wasn't sure what reaction would be appropriate and felt limited by her rudimentary French. Claude took a seat at the head of the table. He rubbed his hands and tucked a napkin into his collar. Lilou found the man almost comical.

Ambroise and Aline took seats next to each other in the middle, and right away started bickering, while Monique circled the room, examining the table. Lilou remained standing, unsure where to sit.

"Please, Lilou, have a seat," Claude said.

She was grateful to have been standing next to a chair diagonal from Aline. It was as far as she could get from her cousin. The seat was right next to the head of the family, and he gave Lilou a thoughtful look. Feeling he was about to ask who she was once again, she prepared to explain to him her relationship to Monique, and that she lived in the United States.

Instead, Claude said, "I must say, I approve of President Pompidou's new policy and the rapprochement with America." His face lit up with a happy smile, as if he'd finally found a topic of conversation that interested him and was also something that others at the lunch table could appreciate.

Lilou nodded vigorously, in an attempt to be as diplomatic as possible. She hated discussing politics and was poorly versed in the subject. Even so, her mother had instilled in her the idea of proper etiquette. Lilou could hear her mother's words in her head. *'You must be able to carry on a conversation on any topic, no matter how absurd or boring. A guest needs to be polite.'*

"So, you agree?" Encouraged, the host continued. "The way I see it, France could learn from the United States, its modernization and economic growth. It's very important to us now. France is a country of great minds, but lately we have lost a lot of ground. We are sister countries, there has always been a certain affinity between France and the US, of course. From the late 1700s, the Revolution, and our desire to modernize and introduce real democracy into the world." Claude coughed and put down his fork. He scanned the faces of his family members for a reaction then stared directly at Lilou.

She averted her eyes. A respectful silence fell over the table. Lilou looked at her empty plate. So focused on the conversation with the host, she had not yet taken a single bite. Aline, clearly used to her father's speeches, had managed to not only get a sizable portion of the quiche, but devoured half of it. Remembering her mother's instructions and pulling all of her French together, Lilou reacted:

"Yes, you're absolutely right! I don't know much about politics, so you must excuse me, but my father also supports the rapprochement between the United States and France under President Nixon. He's very fond of our president." Her cheeks turned crimson, so sure she was that she'd embarrassed herself and would be remembered as the worst guest the family ever had.

"Incroyable![2] Wonderful!" Claude clapped. "This girl is your niece?" He turned to his wife. "How brilliant!"

"Claude, please," Monique admonished her husband.

"Monique, you must agree, this young lady is amazing!" The host looked back at Lilou. "Already, at this young age, so savvy in the political arena. An American, but speaks French with almost no accent. If I had any doubts about our future, I am now convinced. The world will survive!" Claude took his fork and dug his fork into his food. Lilou used the opportunity to serve herself.

The idea of explaining that, in actuality, she understood very little about politics and she merely relayed her father's support for President Nixon occurred to her, but she decided against it, given the content expression on Claude's face. For a few seconds, there was only the sound of silverware clanking, until the host cleared his throat.

"The youth these days! Atrocious. I must say, and it's a real danger to our children, those terrible events of 1968, the punks who poured onto the streets of Paris, a nightmare. The whole world was set back for decades, and France led it into that catastrophe."

Claude was gesticulating wildly now. "A rejection of family values. Those disgusting creatures who decided they knew better than generations of their forefathers, that they didn't want to work and live like we are supposed to. And yet, they feel entitled to everything. A nightmare! Who would have imagined that this type of disaster could happen in France? Who saw it coming? A destruction, total destruction of the way of life and tradition. Of centuries of culture. And this in a country of Voltaire!" His face turned red, and beads of sweat appeared on his forehead.

The family had, once again, stopped eating. Lilou followed suit, despite the grumbling in her stomach.

"Chéri." Lilou heard Monique's voice. There were steely notes in it. "Perhaps I need to get you a sedative?" Auntie Monique stood up and was about to head into the kitchen, but Claude shook his head.

"No, no, my dear, I am just so touched. I know I get overly emotional. You know how I feel about May '68. When I see decency in young people, when I am reminded there are young minds that think for themselves and aren't swayed by these crazy ideas, I know traditional values will prevail." Claude wiped away the tear rolling down his cheek.

Lilou gulped. *Am I really the hope of a generation?* she thought. *If he only knew what I am really like.*

"You see, Lilou, your uncle Claude," Monique smiled with her mouth only, "cares very much about France and its future."

"Uncle? Oh, of course, I am this lady's uncle!" Claude turned to face Lilou, and she almost choked on a piece of quiche that she'd managed to surreptitiously stuff in her mouth. "Young lady, please, tell me, are you studying somewhere? Are you old enough to be in college?"

"Claude, please, don't embarrass her." Monique

rounded her eyes. Aline fidgeted, while Ambroise stared at his plate with such concentration, as if he expected it to offer salvation.

"I would like to know what bright young people study these days. Unlike my own children, who seem to not have any ambition in life whatsoever!" Claude looked at his wife in defiance.

"Claude, please, stop grilling the poor child. Just look at her?" Monique threw her hands up in frustration. Lilou fidgeted in her seat.

Does Monique not know that I am studying to become an accountant? she wondered. "I am going to be an accountant." Lilou's voice sounded hoarse. Remembering the way her junior year had ended and that she would have to finish her finals in September made her uncomfortable, but Lilou also felt pride. Up until her twentieth birthday when she learned of Gary's nuptials, she'd done well in college.

"You see! I knew it!" Claude clapped. "I am glad that you are studying a practical subject like accounting. That's perfect, actually."

"An accountant?" Monique gasped. "But Katrine never mentioned this to me."

"She didn't?" Lilou opened her eyes wide. *Did Maman share anything about me at all?* She tried to conceal her disbelief.

"Not at all. But you have to be good at math to be an accountant, don't you?" Monique rose to reach for the bowl of soup.

"Yes, kind of," Lilou responded. She felt her cheeks redden and felt queasy at the thought of discussing her superior mathematical abilities.

"Monique, why did you hide this gem, this wonderful creature from me all these years? What a great example for Aline, a woman accountant. How brilliant?"

"Claude, darling, please don't forget, you've got the salon tomorrow. I'll make the arrangements," Monique said matter-of-factly. Lilou assumed that the hostess masterfully changed the subject on purpose.

"Tomorrow? Already, but of course! It's here? Our turn to host?" Claude threw a worried look at his wife.

"Yes, darling, I'll take care of everything."

"Perfect, perfect," Claude nodded and turned his attention to his plate.

Lilou expected more questions about accounting, but no one showed any more interest in her studies or plans for the future. After lunch was over, Lilou helped her aunt clear the table. When they were standing in the kitchen, Aline leaning on the sink and Lilou gathering the plates, Auntie Monique announced:

"We are going sightseeing in a little while! Lilou, I hope you are not too tired from the train ride. And it's great that days are longer now as it's still light out even late in the evening."

"Maman always drags us to different churches and squares. You'd think there was nothing else to do in Lyon but go sightseeing!" Aline rumbled.

"Aline, please, we need to show your cousin the city," Monique noted.

"Thank you." The lunch conversation that focused on her person left Lilou with a feeling of unease, and she wanted to ingratiate herself to her aunt.

"No need to thank me. It's your first time in Lyon and it's our duty to show you the city!" Monique smiled and Lilou wondered what kind of woman her aunt really was.

She'd only met Auntie Monique several hours ago, but already the woman seemed to be full of contradictions. Stern mother, doting wife, nature-lover who appreciated modern design trends, hostess who hadn't told her husband about a close relative's visit, and now a generous tour guide.

A woman who, like mother, decided to put an end to twenty seven generations of witchcraft. Lilou swallowed at the thought.

Chapter 12
THE SPELL

It was already late when they returned to the apartment, so Lilou assumed they would go immediately to bed but Monique served dinner. This time they ate in the kitchen, just the three of them, Lilou, her cousin, and her aunt. Ambroise disappeared into his room, and Claude was nowhere to be found. They ate quickly, in silence, and after dinner Lilou retreated to her bedroom, grateful to spend time alone.

She entered the dark bedroom, plopped down on the bed, and stared at the half-open suitcase she'd abandoned earlier that afternoon. The Mary Kay merchandise stared back at her. Lilou jumped up, gasping: *I can't believe I forgot! I was supposed to give these to Auntie Monique. And she must think me so rude to show up empty-handed!* She checked the clock. *After ten in the evening. I really shouldn't put it off until tomorrow.* Lilou grabbed the Mary Kay boxes, slowly opened the door, and crept into the corridor. It was completely dark. *I guess they are asleep;* she thought and froze in place. Lilou heard rustling, and then a voice whispered right into her ear.

"Hey, I was about to come find you!" Aline stepped out of the shadows. "I've got everything ready. We just have to be very quiet. Maman is a light sleeper."

"Ready for what?" Lilou balked and moved back, searching for an escape.

"The spell!" Aline pulled Lilou by the sleeve. "Come on, let's go."

"Where?" Lilou whimpered, but her cousin pushed her into the bedroom and nudged the door shut behind them.

"We are doing the spell tonight. Did you forget?"

"We never agreed—"

"Shh, Maman has insomnia, and if she hears us, I'll be in major trouble!" Aline darted her eyes. "Here, have a seat on the bed!" She pointed, and Lilou obeyed despite her hesitation.

"I am tired, can't we do this another night?" Lilou gulped.

"Tonight is the full moon. We need to take advantage of it!" Aline produced a bag, out of which she took out a candleholder, a black candle, matches, a glass, and a bottle of wine. She examined the items in satisfaction and then fumbled for something in her pocket. "Here it is!" Aline smiled and set a razor next to the empty glass, its sharp edge glistening.

"What's this?" Lilou pulled back. She stood up and moved to the door.

"Don't worry! I know what I'm doing!" Aline smirked. "I am going to be a powerful witch someday. I've got the generational memory! I don't see a downside. We are going to do a spell together, and it'll help you, regardless."

"What spell?" Lilou stared at Aline blankly. Her head began to swim, she felt weak, and the familiar desire to disappear came back.

"A love spell, of course! You told me about your

boyfriend. I saw your face. You aren't sure of him, are you? After we do the love spell, he'll be yours forever!" Aline clapped her hands, as if trapping a fly.

"Gary?" Breath caught in Lilou's throat. "Mine forever?"

"Of course! A love spell is perfect for this kind of thing. He'll be yours *for all eternity*! I promise!" Aline raised her eyebrows. "So, are you ready?" Without waiting for an answer, her cousin lit the candle and then rose to flip the light switch off. Right away, the room took on a sinister appearance, the flickering shadow of the candle on the wall, the brown and green decor of the room adding to its grim appearance.

"Have a seat," Aline instructed, but Lilou remained standing by the door, barely breathing. Aline sat on the bed next to the nightstand and shuffled the objects around. "Voila!" After a moment, there was a popping sound and a vinegary smell filled the room. Aline poured wine into a glass. Lilou's legs felt like cotton candy, and she was sure that they would give in underneath her.

"Now, give me your finger," Aline ordered. As if hypnotized, Lilou walked to her cousin and extended her left hand. Her cousin grabbed her index finger and produced the razor.

Before she knew what was happening, a drop of blood appeared on Lilou's finger. Captivated, Nausea overtook her at the sight of blood, but she forced herself to stare at the tiny crimson drop, while Aline, without saying a word, squeezed the tip of her finger and extracted several drops into the glass of wine. Lilou watched how the blood mixed with the red wine.

"No," Lilou whispered, her voice raw. She looked at Aline, fear gripping her stomach.

"It's not a big deal, and I am going to have to do this

all the time," Aline stated, swirling the concoction. In the candlelight, Aline's head grew horns. Lilou gasped. The girl looked just like Sammy in her nightmare. Lilou remembered Gary, their lost love, the evil fiancée who'd stolen her beloved and a new determination grew inside of Lilou.

I need to do the spell.

"Ready?" Aline looked at her, expectant. Lilou nodded in response. She was now completely at her cousin's disposal. Aline announced, the expression on her face solemn:

"So, here is what you need to do. I wrote out the text of the spell." Aline took out a piece of paper. "Stare at the candle and focus on the flame. And then, you take the glass and read the text out loud." She pointed at the paper.

"Okay." Lilou nodded. She felt as if she were in a classroom, ready for an important exam.

"Your beloved's name is Gary, right?" Aline checked and darted her eyes to the paper.

"Yes," Lilou whispered, "Gary." She loved saying his name. Her one and only true love.

"Here is what you need to say. Repeat it out loud, looking at the candle and then drink the wine in one gulp." Aline handed the paper to Lilou.

> You are my darling and beloved
> We'll be together forever, you and I
> Our hearts are one
> Our blood is wine
> You're caught in my trap
> Don't run, for you're caught

"At the end, you say 'Gary and Lilou, together forever', got it?" Aline scanned Lilou's face.

"Yes," Lilou said softly, enthralled by the beauty of the ritual. She was about to bind her soul together with Gary's forever. *Why didn't I think of doing this before on my own?* Lilou thought. *I could have been with Gary already. I would be the one marrying him!* Lilou stared at the candle, as instructed. She brought the paper closer to her face and read the script out loud. The moment she said 'Gary and Lilou, together forever', Aline handed her the glass and Lilou took a sip.

"No, drink the whole thing!"

"Okay." Lilou finished the wine and felt the room move. The walls merged into one. Lilou tried to put the glass down, but it fell and she heard a crack. As she reached to pick it up, the shadow on the wall grew and formed the shape of Sammy's head. The head opened its vicious mouth, about to absorb her. The next moment it wasn't Sammy's head, but Aline's that had grown fangs. "Ah!" Lilou screamed, and the room went completely dark.

When Lilou opened her eyes, she was on the bed. The candle had gone out and the room was dark. Only faint moonlight shone through the curtain.

"Are you awake?" Aline asked. "Be careful, the glass broke. I picked up the pieces, but there might still be shards on the floor."

"What happened?" Lilou shifted on the bed.

"Everything worked!" Aline hissed. "It was perfect! I knew the full moon was the right time to do this. It was just amazing."

"It was?" Lilou gasped. The idea that Gary would be hers forever drew her in.

"Yes!" Aline drew her chin up. "And I will always remember you as my first client. One day, when I am a world-famous witch and I have clients from all over, I will share this story." Aline raised her voice, gesticulating excitedly.

Lilou felt a knot form in her stomach. Only now did she realize Aline had been experimenting on her.

"But what if something goes wrong? Since it's your first time?"

"Oh, don't worry, it's in my blood!" Aline rose from the bed and began collecting the items she'd brought for the ritual. "And besides, you guys are already together, so it'll just make the relationship stronger. I really don't see why you are so scared."

Lilou felt a lump form in her throat, the image of Gary as he told her about his fiancée appeared.

"See you in the morning." Aline yawned, clutching the bag.

"Good night," Lilou squeezed out, grateful that the strange night was over and she could go to sleep.

Chapter 13
THE SHARD

Lilou woke up to noise outside of her door. A second later, she heard knocking and Aline's head poked inside.

"Good morning! Maman wants to take us on a tour of Lyon!" Aline giggled.

"Another one?" Lilou sat up on the bed and rubbed her eyes. She felt groggy.

"Yes! She wants to leave early, because Papa has his salon this afternoon."

"A salon?" Lilou shifted her weight onto her feet and shrieked in pain. Something sharp dug into her left toe.

"What's wrong?" Aline rushed over.

"Umm, I… I don't know." Lilou turned her foot and saw a shard of glass sticking out.

"Oops, I guess it's from the broken glass. I probably missed it last night." Aline stared at Lilou's foot in wonder.

Lilou felt nausea rise in her stomach. Drops of blood formed as she pulled at the glass.

"No, let me do it." Aline reached as Lilou shrieked again. "You have to be fast, like this." Aline got the glass out. It was long and narrow. "It's nothing, see?"

The cut did look small. "Yeah," Lilou mumbled, staring at her foot.

"Maybe I can become a healer, too! Not just a witch!" A smug smile crossed Aline's face. "Come on, we have to get ready. Maman wants us to come back at eleven. Papa brings his friends over, they spend time together, talk about politics, it's super boring." Aline moved to the door. "I gotta go get ready. See you in the kitchen." She slammed the door behind her, leaving Lilou sitting on the bed.

Lilou grazed some spit over the cut, then sighed and put on socks and got dressed.

At breakfast, which consisted of a baguette and hot chocolate, Lilou tried her best to smile and be as pleasant as possible. She fought the feeling of sadness that overwhelmed her. A premonition of something terrible happening loomed over her. Her life felt a failure, and she was a waste of space, a mere dot in the infinite universe. Her only reason for existence, her Gary, was no longer hers, and her pathetic effort to return him had failed.

ON THE TOUR of the city, Lilou barely paid attention. She followed her aunt, feeling numb, while Monique told the story of Lyon. They entered a church that had been built in the 8th or 9th century and had been rebuilt many times since. Monique spoke about architecture, about the Gothic style, about symbolism, but Lilou could not bring herself to pay attention. Rather, she wanted to cower in a corner and hide. The world felt gray again, a sad and unhappy place. Lilou thought of the futility of being.

With a feeling of disdain, Lilou looked at her chipper cousin and felt a bitter disappointment. *Why did I let her burn the candle and perform that stupid ritual? I should have gone to sleep! Kicked her out of the room, told her I wasn't interested. I should have known better!*

Aline, completely oblivious to Lilou's suffering, buzzed nearby. They passed yet another church, walked on an adorable cobblestone street, and Auntie Monique pointed out the street's unique features, but Lilou felt as if in a fog. Aline chattered on. There were passersby, life went on, and Lilou felt bile rising in her throat. She was an outsider. She did not belong in this happy, bright world. The memory of what she and Aline had done the night before added to a wave of nausea that came over her. Lilou felt sick and stopped, leaning on the wall of a building.

"Lilou, what's wrong?" Her aunt ran up to her. "Aline, stop talking. Your cousin doesn't feel well."

"I am okay," Lilou squeezed out.

"Oh, poor dear, let's head home! It must be the weather, it's so hot these days. We can finish sightseeing later." Auntie Monique checked the time, and the beautiful golden bracelet of her watch glimmered in the sun. "Oh, dear, would you look at the time? We should be heading back anyway. I need time to set up for the salon."

On the way to the car, Lilou gnawed at herself. *I shouldn't have done the spell.* The thought swirled in her head, insistent and worrisome. Regret felt good and familiar and the sadness that overcame her pulled Lilou in. The more she felt regret, the lower her spirits got. By the time they got back to the apartment, Lilou wanted only one thing: to hide.

"Auntie Monique, I am sorry. Is it okay if I go lie down?" Lilou mumbled.

"Of course, dear, please do. Have some water." Monique pointed toward the kitchen.

Shoulders slumped, Lilou went to the kitchen to pour herself a glass of water and carried it to the bedroom. She set it on the nightstand, in the same spot where the glass of wine stood the night before. Immediately, a flashback of the ritual hit her. *Not that again!* Lilou thought, and leaned on the bed. She took a sip of water, laid down, and closed her eyes.

She woke up to the sound of voices outside the door, clattering. It sounded as if furniture was being moved. Auntie Monique was giving orders to Aline and Ambroise. *I can't be rude to the hosts. I should probably go out and say hello,* she thought. Though her head felt foggy and her limbs were heavy, she forced herself to get up.

The moment she stood, she yelped, feeling a throbbing pain in her left foot. She took off her sock to examine it. Her big toe had turned deep purple. Closing her eyes, she willed the swelling and pain to go away, but it was as if all of her body was now concentrated in one spot. The pain felt sharper and was now shooting through her heel. Lilou brushed her fingers over her foot and it was hot to the touch. Hobbling to the door, she peaked into the corridor. She heard the clinking of glasses. *The salon must have started,* Lilou realized. She threw a panicked look around the room.

"Hey, how are you?" Aline appeared out of the shadows.

How does she do that?

"I need to see a doctor," Lilou whispered urgently, feeling drops of cold sweat on her forehead.

"A doctor? Why? Let's go to the kitchen. Papa's salon is in full swing, so we gotta be quiet."

"I don't think I can wait, the shard of glass, I need help." Lilou suddenly wanted to cry. "Remember, you pulled it out this morning? I think it was infected. I might get gangrene and die!"

"Are you for real? There is no way that's going to happen. Just wait. Papa will be done in a few hours."

"It's bad." There were hysterical notes in Lilou's voice.

"Let me see." Aline leaned over as Lilou raised her foot from the floor, leaning on her right side. It was dark in the corridor, but the swelling of the left side was visible. Aline assessed the situation. "Oh it looks nasty."

"I know," Lilou squealed. She felt tears well up in her eyes, while at the same time, a desire to punch Aline rose in her. *It's all her fault. If it weren't for the stupid spell, that dumb wine and the glass, I wouldn't have had any problems. Now I might end up in a hospital!*

"Let me feel it." Before Lilou could stop the girl, Aline reached for her toe and Lilou shrieked in pain. As Lilou tried to put the injured foot down gently, she lost her balance and ended up stepping on the raw left foot. The sudden pressure made the pain unbearable, and Lilou released a deep howl. Auntie Monique appeared in the corridor as if on cue. She was wearing a bright orange dress, her hair was in a 'do', an overall look festive.

"What's happening here? Aline, why aren't you in your room? You know the rules. When Papa has his salon, you must be a good girl and stay out of the away." Auntie Monique turned to Lilou and opened her eyes wide. Lilou bit her lower lip, no longer able to conceal her pain. "What's wrong?" The woman hissed.

"I, I need to see a doctor. I am sorry," Lilou mumbled, staring at the floor. "It's my toe."

"Your toe?" Auntie Monique exclaimed.

"I think it might get infected and I'll get gangrene!" Lilou said. She remembered stories of wounded soldiers' infected limbs her father told her and felt a knot form in her stomach. "It hurts so much!" She lifted her foot to show her aunt, and the woman stepped back.

"Oh, that looks terrible. What happened?" Monique scanned Lilou's face and turned her attention to Aline. "Is there something I should know?"

"No, Maman, I don't know anything," Aline mumbled.

"Let's go to the kitchen, so I can see what's going on," Monique said. Aline stayed behind, while Lilou followed her aunt. "Show me," Monique ordered, and Lilou obediently lifted her foot on the tabouret. "How did this happen?"

"I don't know." Lilou felt her cheeks turn red. Lying did not come easily to her, and she felt a deep embarrassment. "But it hurts badly." That was the truth, the pain was unbearable.

"It might be a splinter, hold on a second," Monique said and left the kitchen. Lilou sat down on the stool, stretching her leg. She stared at her throbbing foot, feeling dread. Moments later, just as Lilou began thinking about the futility of her trip to France and the sad loss of Gary, Monique appeared, followed by a young man. He wasn't tall, but moved confidently with the stature of someone used to regular physical activity.

"Didier, this is my niece, Lilou. She is the American girl I mentioned. I am sorry I interrupted the salon, but I am worried about her. She seems to have cut her foot." Monique pursed her lips.

"I didn't know you had a niece, how lovely to meet her." The man's voice sounded pleasant and soft.

"Katrine, my sister, lives in the United States, in a small city, Pittsburgh, and this is her daughter. The poor girl is in a lot of pain."

"Of course. Let me take a look. I didn't bring my tools, so I might have to take your niece to my office." The young man stepped closer and Lilou saw his face.

His eyes were a vivid shade of blue, so bright that Lilou

felt as if they could blind her. He had thick brown hair and a straight nose. A masculine chin. Lilou felt shock pass through her body. He was very attractive. *But Gary is the only man in my life*, flashed through her mind, as she averted her eyes to stare at the floor.

"Didier Lambert," the man said and extended his hand. Their eyes met and Lilou blushed. She felt a spark light inside of her. *But I am just dreaming*, she brushed the idea off.

"Nice to meet you, I am Lilou." She squeezed out and felt her cheeks turn an even deeper shade of red. *I am pathetic, this is awful.*

"What an interesting name for an American? And you speak great French," Didier noted.

"Um, I…" Lilou mumbled incoherently.

"She does speak great French. Didier, I am so sorry, but I am sure that my husband would like for you to return to the salon. I think it will just take a moment. Lilou, please, show your foot to the doctor," Monique fussed.

"Of course." Didier nodded at Monique and then turned to Lilou. "May I see your foot? Let's place it right here." He pointed at another stool and pushed it toward Lilou. Now she was sitting with her leg raised. Staring at the pale skin of her leg, she felt incredibly self-conscious.

"Very good, very good, I just need to wash my hands." The doctor scanned the space in search of a sink.

"The soap is right here. I should have thought of it earlier." Monique shook her head.

Didier quickly headed to the sink and then said in a firm voice, "Great, now I am ready."

As if by magic, Monique fluttered away leaving Lilou with the handsome doctor. She stared at the floor in front of her, too terrified to lift her eyes at Didier. Immediately forgetting all about the throbbing pain, the risk of gangrene, the infected toe, her lost love for Gary, the memory of the spell, and her resentment against Aline. All of it disappeared, to be replaced by this man.

Didier Lambert squatted next to her as he gently adjusted her foot. "

"Does that hurt?" He touched her foot. His hands were warm and soft and his touch made Lilou suck in her breath. "If I push like this?"

"No," Lilou murmured.

"And like this?" The doctor pressed the swollen spot on her big toe.

"Ouch! Oh!" Lilou shrieked in pain, unable to control herself. She jerked her foot and nearly kicked the man and immediately scanned his face to see if her actions had upset him.

"I am sorry, just one second." Didier rose and looked to the door, where Monique stood, observing. Lilou having all but forgotten about her aunt's existence, noticed the woman with surprise.

"Is there anything that you need?" Monique cocked her head to the side and looked like a bird, eager to please, but also ready to peck, if necessary.

I wonder if she finds him attractive? Lilou felt a pang of jealousy.

"Just something sharp. Maybe a needle? There is a splinter and I need to get it out immediately."

"Of course, right away." Monique sprinted off, leaving Lilou alone in the kitchen with the handsome man.

"Don't worry, you'll be all better soon." He gave Lilou a reassuring smile. He did not move his eyes away, but continued to look at her, as if asking her the question: *Do you like me?* Lilou swallowed hard and internally responded with a 'yes'. Once more, she felt her cheeks turn red.

"Here you are!" Monique appeared with a sewing box.

"What size do you need?" She spouted out, opening the box and producing a small needle.

"Thicker, please," the doctor responded, and Lilou's eyes widened in horror.

"Don't worry, it will be over soon." The man squeezed her hand and the softness of his touch calmed Lilou down. A second later, he rose, and Lilou wished for him to return to her side, so comfortable she felt next to him. "Do you have any iodine? Or peroxide? And I'll need clean water and a bandage. I will disinfect the needle right here." He turned to the stove and turned it on.

"Why?" Lilou gasped.

"Fire kills off bacteria, better than anything else."

"Oh," Lilou nodded. The doctor waved the needle over the open fire and a second later, he squatted next to her again. His presence next to her felt so comforting that Lilou wanted to purr with pleasure.

"So, let's do this. Are you ready?" The tone of his voice was delicate and considerate. *I am just imagining this,* Lilou told herself. "I will get the splinter out and you'll be all set," Didier said, and Lilou felt as if the man had just professed his love for her. She averted her eyes, afraid to be disappointed yet again, but then she felt his stare.

She looked up and saw that Didier was looking straight at her and then he smiled. In his smile, she read all that she needed to know. It was what she'd wanted from Gary, what she'd expected from her neighbor. Genuine interest. All of her questions had been answered. *It feels good to have a guy like you first!* Lilou thought.

At that moment, she understood that her feelings for Gary were nothing but her imagination. Something incredible was unfolding in front of her very eyes, developing fast, furiously, quickly, and it could not be stopped. A new love story, maybe even a happy one, was enveloping Lilou and pulling her in. And in this story, she would be the one accepting love, not the other way around.

"So, how is it going?" Monique's voice reached her from far away.

"Going great, almost done." Didier cleared his throat, and Lilou understood that for him it was difficult to be pulled away from her. "We just need a few more minutes," he added, and the intimate 'we' that he used caused a flutter in Lilou's stomach. *I am imagining this. This can't be real!* She tried to force herself to stop, but the pull of Didier was too strong.

"Of course, I'll be waiting outside," Monique said, closing the door behind her.

What's happening? Lilou opened her eyes wide.

"Listen, don't worry, I'll make it quick, you won't even know what happened." He looked at her and Lilou blushed as if the doctor had said something indecent. Didier pressed her toe, stuck in the needle and after a second pulled out a thin and long shard of glass. Lilou gasped. "Here! Look at that thing! Incredible, I wonder how it got into your toe. And how did you even manage to walk?"

"That was in my foot? I can't believe it!" Lilou stared at the shard. It was nearly an inch long. Didier picked up iodine and generously spread it over the wound.

"Listen, can you come see me tomorrow? In my office?" He deftly bandaged her toe. Lilou felt no pain, she was so absorbed in this man, so enthralled by his interest in her.

"Tomorrow?" Lilou cleared her throat. Going to see him the next day meant they would now be separated. But that would be hard, because being with Didier felt so good.

"Yes, tomorrow morning, at the office. Monique knows where it is. She can bring you."

"Of course." Lilou nodded.

"Then I'll see you tomorrow," Didier said and then gently squeezed her hand. Before Lilou could react, he pulled away and moved to the sink. There was a sound of water and then the door opened and Monique walked into the kitchen. Lilou felt frozen in place. She could not move, could not get up, and she watched as her aunt thanked Didier, who nodded in her direction and then walked out of the kitchen.

Did that all just happen? Lilou looked around her. *I must have dreamt it all. There is no way that could have happened. Didier*, Lilou moaned softly. She wanted to close her eyes and picture his face, think about him, dream about being next to him again, but a second later she heard a muffled dialogue. It was her aunt and the doctor speaking in the corridor. Bits of the conversation reached her ears, and Lilou listened, careful not to miss anything.

"Monique, please bring your niece tomorrow to see me. I pulled out a splinter, so sharp and long, I don't know how the poor girl could stand it."

"Of course, your office? What time tomorrow?"

"We open at nine, so come before, let's say, eight in the morning?"

"Yes, we'll be there."

"Perfect." Didier cleared his throat. There was a sound of something rustling and Lilou shifted in her seat, trying to make sure she didn't miss anything the doctor was saying.

"So, is it serious? Her foot? She'll be alright?"

"Oh yes, don't worry. I just want to make sure the infection doesn't spread." Hearing this, Lilou's heart sank. The terrible stories her father told her of his friends dying from their wounds pierced her consciousness once more.

She pushed away the frightening thought and continued to listen.

"I am so sorry, Didier. I really didn't think that we would make such an unreasonable demand on your time. You are so kind! Really, we owe you a great debt," Monique said, her tone once again regaining the obsequious notes that made Lilou cringe.

"Oh, Monique, please, it's my pleasure. Medicine is my calling in life. And I've taken the Hippocratic oath. Who would I be if I didn't treat a patient in need and instead chose to socialize with friends, no matter how esteemed?"

He is such a great man! Lilou concluded, hearing Didier's words. A moment later, Lilou heard a door open and the sound of glass clanking. Loud conversation reached her ears. She shifted in her seat to look at her foot then leaned on her right side to get up.

"Lilou, I think you should be resting. The doctor said that you had a serious splinter, a huge piece of glass." Monique walked into the kitchen and rushed to her side. "It's quite dangerous. I am going to have to have a chat with our maid, because really, where would a shard of glass like that come from? And maybe she broke something and didn't tell me. You can never be too careful." Monique's face took on a belligerent expression that contrasted with her adorable blue eyes and button nose. "Let me help you to your room, Lilou. You must be exhausted." Monique gave Lilou a look full of meaning, and Lilou understood it was time for her to disappear until the salon had ended.

"Of course, thank you, I will be okay." Lilou hobbled along, dragging the left foot behind her. The bandage made it difficult to step on it.

"I'll call you for dinner, have some rest for now," Monique said and fluttered off toward the salon. With a bit of effort, Lilou entered her room and sat on the bed.

She then remembered that she hadn't closed the door, rose with a sigh, and limped to the door. Just as she was about to close it, Aline peaked in.

"Hey, is it true? You had a huge splinter? I heard the doctor talk to Maman."

At the sight of her cousin, Lilou sighed, "Aline, I need to rest. Let's talk later, please."

Ignoring her, Aline walked in, then bent over Lilou's foot to stare at the bandage. "I thought we pulled out all the glass. I don't get it."

"Aline, please," Lilou begged, but her cousin paid her no attention.

"Listen, please make sure you don't say anything to my mom, because then I'll be in big trouble. And I don't want any problems because I was helping you."

"What?" Lilou opened her eyes wide. "You? Helping me?"

"Of course I was. I hope that you are grateful." Aline shook her head.

"The way I see it, I was helping you! I didn't even want to do the stupid spell!" Lilou shrieked.

"Oh, as if. You were all over the spell, just dying for your Gary. And once you go back there, you'll see. My magic is very powerful!" Aline crossed her arms, staring at Lilou with judgment.

"I don't even want any magic! I don't like this stuff!"

"Just trust me, embrace it. It's beautiful and powerful. And once grandmother transfers her powers to me, once I've been initiated," Aline smiled dreamily, "I'll be the most famous witch in all of France!"

"Aline, this is ridiculous. None of this stuff is real! I don't even understand why you'd want to be a witch!" Lilou shook her head. She leaned back and sat on the bed.

Her head spun, and Lilou put her hand down to stabilize herself.

"Why I'd want to be a witch? Why *wouldn't* I want to be one? The moment I learned about our grandmother and hereditary powers, I knew I'd be the one. I was never good at school, I hate math, always wondering what I'd do in life. Other than marrying a rich guy, because that's not that interesting. But once I heard about the generations of witches in our family, I knew I'd be one, too. I will make them all proud. I am just waiting for Grand-mère to pass the powers to me." Aline stared across the room with a dreamy look on her face.

"You don't think it's wrong?" Lilou furrowed her brow.

"Of course not! Witchcraft helps people, and just think, it can make the bond between you and this Gary stronger. How's that wrong?" Aline shrugged.

"But what if I don't want him?"

"Oh, well, in that case, it'll probably just go away." Aline waved her hand indefinitely.

"Alright, I guess you are right." Lilou frowned. Thinking about the spell and its consequences made her feel uneasy, and she wanted to push the unpleasant thoughts away.

"You worry too much!" Aline wrinkled her nose. "I guess it's because you are going to be an accountant. That's some serious work." She let out a giggle.

"I guess," Lilou conceded. "By the way, who was the doctor? The guy who treated me just now. Do you know him?" Lilou made her voice sound as expressionless as possible to conceal the strong desire to learn about the magnetic man she'd just met. The pull to him was incredibly strong, despite the very short time they had spent together.

"I don't really know. I don't pay attention to those

people. He seems boring, just like the rest of Papa's friends." Aline sighed.

"Boring? I thought he was nice."

"He's just like all of Papa's friends, only interested in politics. Who cares, anyway?"

"He seemed like a good doctor," Lilou said. "I've to go see him tomorrow."

"Yeah, that sucks for you. Instead of enjoying your vacation, you gotta run around with all this medical stuff." Aline gave Lilou an assessing look, as if trying to measure her cousin's potential to enjoy life.

Chapter 14
THE DOCTOR

That night, Lilou dreamed of a forest. The one from her dream while staying with her grandparents. Wolfgang, the wolf, was by her side. Her guardian and protector. She walked at a steady pace, moving fast through the trees, and he kept pace. They did not speak but held a comfortable silence between them. Lilou knew the wolf would do anything to protect her.

They crossed valleys and climbed mountains, passing lush trees and bright green spaces. Flowers bloomed and birds chirped. It was a magical place, with shades of dark purple and deep violet crossing the emerald greenery. Lilou felt at complete peace with the world. Such a beautiful and magical dream, that the sound of her alarm could not interrupt it. Instead, the alarm turned into a parakeet atop one of the tree branches which made a noise Lilou tried to recognize.

"Lilou, Lilou, time to wake up." She heard a woman's voice and jerked up. There was a knock on the door, and the next moment, Auntie Monique walked into the bedroom. "Good morning, Lilou, it's time to get ready. You have a doctor's appointment." Monique wore a beautiful summer dress, white with red flowers.

Lilou sat up and rubbed her eyes. She remembered her toe and wiggled her left foot, then leaned over to look at it. She pulled back the bandage. The toe was still red but no longer as swollen as it had been the day before.

"Good morning." Lilou climbed out of the bed.

"How is your foot? Better?" Auntie Monique gave Lilou's foot a cursory look and then ordered: "We leave in thirty minutes. Didier asked us to be there at eight, so we need to hurry."

"Is Aline coming?" Lilou asked.

"No, not this time. I am letting her sleep in. And the visit will be a short one. I think we'll be back by nine." Monique nodded at her niece. "Breakfast is in the kitchen. I'll see you there." She exited the room, closing the door behind her firmly.

Lilou got dressed, still avoiding leaning on her injured foot, though she did not feel the acute pain any longer. The memory of her dream and the magical forest was gone, as if it never happened.

A few minutes later, Lilou was sitting at the kitchen table with a bowl of hot chocolate and a piece of baguette in front of her. At the center of the table, there sat butter and strawberry jam. Already used to the French breakfast, Lilou eagerly spread butter on the baguette. She remembered her mother's words about the superiority of French food and internally disagreed with her mother's assessment. In Lilou's opinion, French breakfast was not superior to American breakfast. She would have much rather preferred heartier food in the morning. Lilou wolfed down the food in front of her in several large bites and was left wanting more. She scanned the kitchen, hoping for something else to eat, when her aunt walked in.

"Are you ready? Oh you look much better, I must say." Monique gave her an assessing look. "Maybe we skip the visit?"

At that moment, Lilou remembered Didier. She thought of their introduction, the splinter, his soft hands, how his gaze lingered on her just a little too long. "Oh but what if there is something serious? And I am so afraid of gangrene!" Lilou tried to twist her face in pain.

"Of course, of course, Katrine will kill me if I send you back with an infection," her aunt mumbled. "Let's go then. He will be waiting for us."

"Auntie Monique, I wanted to tell you. I am sorry. It was me who broke the glass." Lilou cleared her throat as soon as they got in the car. She was waiting for the right moment to tell Monique about the glass, and decided this was the best opportunity she would ever get, since they weren't facing each other.

"You did?"

"I was just clumsy, I am sorry." Lilou turned red. She thought she saw her aunt narrow her eyes.

"Thank you for letting me know." Aunt Monique responded gingerly. "I am glad it wasn't serious. And that it wasn't the maid. It's such a hassle to find a new one."

It didn't take long to reach Didier's office. Lilou stayed silent on the way, while Monique hummed a tune Lilou did not recognize. They got out of the car in front of a plain building with the sign 'Cabinet medical'. *That must be it.* Lilou's heart leaped at the thought that she would soon see Didier. The door was unlocked, and they entered the empty waiting room.

"I guess he opened early for us." Monique took a seat and placed her purse on her lap. Lilou stood, leaning on the counter. The office door opened and Didier appeared. He wore a white doctor's coat and Lilou caught a whiff of his cologne. It smelled fresh and pleasant, making her head spin.

"Monique, thank you for bringing your niece over." Didier leaned over and kissed Monique three times. *I must have imagined the whole thing,* she thought. *He probably just wanted to see Monique. I guess that's why she's so dressed up.* The terrible thought pierced her imagination.

"Thank you for opening early for us, Doctor." Monique let out a giggle. Lilou swallowed hard.

"Welcome, welcome," he said. Turning to Lilou, Didier asked: "How are you feeling today?" He looked at her with such tenderness and care that all her doubts immediately dissipated.

"Much better, doctor," she whispered, averting her eyes.

"I am glad to hear that," he said and, for a brief moment, Lilou was sure that he would now tell her to leave, since she'd been healed. But Didier Lambert gave her a soft smile and said: "Let's take a closer look at your foot, shall we?" Without waiting for an answer, he opened the office door and gestured for Lilou to enter. Her aunt stayed behind, while Lilou limped inside.

"Have a seat right here." He pointed to a cot. Lilou obediently climbed up and waited. The doctor washed his hands and there was a rattling of instruments. *Maybe I imagined it all.* Lilou felt panic rise in her throat yet again.

"Your foot?" He turned to Lilou.

"Oh, yes, sorry." Lilou blushed. She took off her shoe.

Didier took her foot in his hands, sending a shiver through Lilou's body. His fingers were warm, and she wanted him to keep touching her, to caress her, to continue up her leg and thigh. He took off the bandage that Lilou had hastily reapplied after showering that morning and, as he did this, Lilou took the opportunity to inspect him. She noticed that his hair was a light shade of brown and there were small wrinkles on his forehead.

"It is healing nicely," Didier announced after a few seconds. He applied iodine again, then applied a clean bandage. "I am glad I got to treat you yesterday," he added after a pause.

Lilou reached for her shoe. "Thank you for your help, Doctor," she said. *I guess it's now or never if he's going to ask to see me again,* Lilou thought, looking up at Didier.

"I know that this isn't the right thing, but I believe that in life we are given certain opportunities." The doctor cleared his throat. "I am not supposed to get involved with my patients, but it's only a minor wound, so you won't be my patient after today. And I gave it some thought, I actually didn't sleep well last night." Didier looked at Lilou. "I felt a genuine connection between us, something strong that brought us together," he added after a pause.

With each word, Lilou felt as if she were melting, sinking deeper and deeper into something incredible. It was her own fairy tale, the one she'd been waiting for. The one that she tried to create with Gary, but in vain. *So this is what it should feel like!* Flashed in her mind.

"What do you think?" Didier asked, looking into her eyes.

"What do I think?" Lilou repeated. Her throat felt parched and her lips were dry.

"Would you like to see each other again?" He ran his hand through his hair and laughed: "Not here, of course."

"Oh, yes!" She nodded.

"Perfect!" Didier smiled, and it lit up his whole face. He reached for her hand.

He is so handsome! Lilou thought, staring at the doctor. "But, I am leaving on Friday, and then I am flying back to Pittsburgh," Lilou mumbled, suddenly jerking back to reality.

"I thought about that. I know we have little time, but I believe one must seize the day. I knew there was a reason we met. There was a reason you had that strange splinter." Didier announced. "Let's meet tonight? Would you like that?"

"Of course, I would love to!" Lilou responded. "But what about my hosts?" She pictured her cousin's curious and mocking face, and her heart sank at the thought of Aline's judgment.

"Don't worry, I'll take care of everything. Please tell me you want to see me again," Didier urged. "That's all that matters," he added, looking at her intently.

"Yes, I do, I want to see you again," Lilou responded.

"I'll pick you up at seven tonight," Didier said, still holding her hand in his. Lilou rose from the cot and they were now standing next to each other. She noticed that, unlike Gary, who was much taller, she and Didier were almost the same height. Despite that, next to Didier, she felt protected. They exited the office together, with Didier's hand on the small of her back, and Lilou reveling in his attention.

"Monique, I wanted to speak to you for a moment," the doctor said to her aunt.

"Sure." The woman gave the two of them a quick glance over and smiled, and at that moment Lilou realized Monique must have suspected something all along.

"Monique, I'd like to see Lilou tonight, and have dinner with her," Didier said.

"Of course," Monique nodded, "But please tell Claude about your plans."

"I will." Didier nodded. "And I must say, you don't

have to worry. My intentions are serious," the doctor said with grave notes in his voice.

"I assumed that was the case," Monique smiled.

"I'll see you tonight, then," Didier said to Monique and, turning to Lilou, added, "See you soon." He then kissed her on the cheek, and the intimacy of their touch made Lilou blush.

As she and Monique exited the office, Lilou noticed the time. It was eight twenty-five. Only twenty five minutes to completely shift her reality. The events of her life unfolding with an incredible speed around her, and she was only an observer, rather than a participant.

"Lilou, relax, he is just a man," Monique noted as they walked to the car.

"Oh, I, umm," Lilou stuttered, looking over at her aunt, unable to speak. They got into the car.

"Try not to be so tense when you see him tonight," Monique said, starting the car. She looked over at Lilou and gave her a reassuring smile.

"Yes, I will try," Lilou nodded, and, having regained the power of speech, added, "It's just so sudden, and I really didn't expect something like this to happen!" Lilou felt tears in her eyes. Tears of joy. A beautiful thing was about to happen to her. A good man had expressed interest in her, and had 'serious intentions'. She felt noticed and appreciated, and it was happening in real life, and not in her head.

"That's the beauty of love! It happens when you least expect it!" Monique smiled softly. "Didier is a good man, a widower. Poor guy."

"A widower!" Lilou let out a cry.

"Yes, it's a tragic story. He isn't even thirty yet, got married five years ago, a pretty girl, but turned out she had a problem with alcohol. A few months after they got married, she started having issues. And him a doctor, imagine how he suffered."

"That sounds terrible!" A picture formed in Lilou's head. Didier with a pained expression on his face next to a beautiful woman, who was chugging down a bottle of champagne.

"Yes, a terrible story, and this girl drank herself to death, literally. Liver failure, and at her age. She was barely twenty-five."

"I don't know what to say." Lilou stared at the road in front of her. Feeling happy over the loss of Didier's wife was wrong, but at the same time, if it weren't for this woman's untimely death, Lilou would not have had any prospects with the handsome doctor.

"Oh, I am sure he's over it now. You know, we tried introducing him two years back, soon after it all happened, and he just wouldn't agree to anything. So sad, we thought he'd remain a bachelor forever."

"I see." Lilou turned to face her aunt.

"So it's quite unexpected, but I am pleased. Claude and I, we care for Didier. He is a good man, and a very talented doctor. But of course, you saw it for yourself."

"But I am leaving!" Lilou let out a cry.

"Oh, if it's love, anything is possible!"

"But how would I know if it's real love?" Lilou asked, feeling desperate now. She felt lost and sought answers from her aunt, forgetting that they barely knew each other, and that only the day prior, her aunt seemed distant and unpleasant.

"If it's love, you won't question it. You'll just know." Monique chuckled.

"Ummm," Lilou hummed, unable to formulate a response.

"Just give Didier a chance. And it's really something

that women forget, but let him express himself. Let *him* win you over. He is the man, so he needs to show that he is worthy of you."

Lilou stared at her aunt, who was holding the steering wheel firmly and looking at a distance. *I always thought it was the other way around,* Lilou pondered. *Did I have it all wrong?*

"You choose, you are the woman, *you* decide if you want a man. A man gets a lot more from a woman in a relationship and marriage. And in order to get to that point, the man has to earn a woman's love. Didn't my sister tell you this?"

"Maman? Kind of." Lilou stammered. She remembered her mother's words on her twentieth birthday, as she sobbed in her bed. *Did that count as advice about men and relationships? Was that enough?*

"How about we get you ready for your date?" Auntie Monique smiled at her niece.

Chapter 15
THE DATE

The rest of the day, Lilou spent in a daze under the watchful eye of her aunt. The air around her had been transformed, and she was breathing love. Lilou did not know how Aline found out about the date with Didier, but as soon as she returned to the apartment, her cousin appeared in the doorway of her bedroom.

"Are you really going on a date with him?"

"Yes." Lilou averted her eyes, trying to sound as vague as possible.

"What about Gary, your beloved?" Aline raised her eyebrows.

"Well, he isn't here, is he?" Lilou shrugged. She had forgotten all about Gary. Her suffering, the years of yearning for Gary, had disappeared without a trace the moment Didier came into the picture.

"You're crazy!" Aline giggled. "I didn't know you were like that. I kinda took you for a dork." Lilou frowned so Aline immediately rushed to correct herself. "I don't mean a dork, but you know, I thought you were serious. And then the spell. So, I figured you really wanted the guy. I dunno."

"The spell had been your idea!" Lilou protested.

"Alright, alright, I guess it doesn't matter. But this doctor, he's older, like he's friends with Papa!" Aline announced with judgment in her voice.

"He is not even thirty. That's not too old." Lilou had already done a calculation in her head. "My dad is eight years older than my mom, and it's worked out for them just fine."

"Are you saying you're gonna marry the guy? I thought you'd just go on one date." Aline tilted her head, giving Lilou a curious look.

"I don't know," Lilou responded, resentment building against her all-knowing cousin.

"Well, anyway, I guess you need to look good for your date!" Aline opined. "Maman said she will help you."

"Yes." Lilou nodded. She thought about her own mother, and the fact that the two of them never had the occasion to get Lilou ready for a date and, despite herself, felt the corners of her mouth droop.

"Hey, why are you all sad? It's okay, don't worry so much. Or are you afraid because he is French? I am sure French guys are just like American ones, you got nothing to worry about!" Aline reassured her.

Lilou laughed. "How do you know so much about men?" she asked Aline.

"I watch a lot of movies!" Her cousin noted wisely. "Anyway, what are you going to wear?" Aline glanced at Lilou's suitcase and then, without waiting for a response, squatted down next to it and started ruffling through Lilou's clothes.

"Hey, stop it," Lilou protested.

Aline pulled out a red shirt, shook it out and handed to Lilou. "You can wear this one. I have a skirt you can borrow."

"I have my own!" Lilou responded.

"No way! That's ridiculous, that long thing?" Aline pointed at Lilou's favorite long, brown skirt that she had worn on their day of sightseeing.

"Or you can wear a dress? Do you have any cute ones?"

"This one?" Lilou took out a navy blue dress that her mother had packed for her. She had a flashback to a hot afternoon spent at a store, when she tried on what seemed like hundreds of outfits, while her mother watched, cigarette in hand, and would indicate her approval by a nod or disapproval by pursing her lips.

"Oh, no way, that's too somber for a date. You'll look like you are going to a funeral. I'll be right back," Aline promised and disappeared. She returned a few minutes later with two skirts. "Here you go!" The girl handed them to Lilou who gulped as she took them. They were mini-skirts, the kind that would come to the middle of her thigh. She'd seen girls wear them in Paris, and even in Pittsburgh, but Lilou had never thought of dressing like that herself.

"I can't wear these!" She protested, shaking her head. "I won't look good."

"Oh, come on! Don't be all modest, that's just silly."

"But it's not me, I dress differently." Lilou moved back, leaving the skirts on the bed.

"You need to look good for that date, so just pick one. They are brand new. I only got them a few weeks ago with Maman. And I think we are the same size, so you are lucky." Aline looked at her. "But if you won't even try them on, I'll take them back." She added after Lilou didn't answer.

Lilou stared at the two skirts, not knowing which one to pick first.

"Here, just try this on." Aline handed her the dark orange skirt. "It'll look alright with the red top."

"Thank you." Lilou grabbed the skirt and held it up. She expected her cousin to leave, but Aline did not move and continued standing in the middle of the bedroom. "Are you going to stay?"

"Yeah, what are you, shy?" Aline shrugged. "It's not a big deal, just a skirt." She rolled her eyes.

Lilou started to undress, feeling goosebumps on her legs under Aline's watchful gaze. Lilou pulled on the miniskirt and checked herself out in the mirror. Her legs looked long and the skirt fit her well. *Aline is being kind, I need to be more gracious,* Lilou thought.

"Maybe this wasn't such a good idea, your legs are so pale," Aline said gingerly.

"Oh, I guess they are." Lilou stared at her skin, now painfully aware of the pallor of her skin. *I guess she isn't that kind after all,* Lilou thought of her cousin.

"You could wear pantyhose, but you'll be hot," Aline added with a vindictive smile. Before she could continue, Monique appeared in the doorway.

"Oh, how pretty you look, Lilou. Aline, thank you for sharing your clothes." She turned to her daughter.

Was it Auntie Monique's idea to have me wear the mini-skirt? Lilou wondered.

"Lilou, I'll help you apply make-up. Please come to my boudoir." Monique led Lilou down the corridor. The door to it had always been locked, and it was the first time Lilou entered it. Spacious, though still smaller than the room Lilou's parents shared in Pittsburgh. A vanity stood by the window. Monique gestured for Lilou to sit and produced a whole stack of small boxes and powders.

Lilou noticed the Mary Kay boxes her mother had sent sitting in the corner, still sealed. She had managed to remember them and presented her aunt with the make-up after the salon had ended. Monique applied a powder on Lilou's cheeks, and Lilou's face acquired a healthy, bright complexion. She then made Lilou close her eyes and Lilou felt a soft brush on her eye lids. A few minutes later, Lilou was wearing eyeliner and eyeshadow, but her face looked natural, bright, and healthy. She liked what she saw.

"Thank you," she said, turning her face left and right.

"You look perfect! I am sure Didier will find you irresistible!"

He arrived at her hosts' apartment exactly at 7pm. Claude was only slightly confused by the fact that his young friend was taking his niece somewhere on a date. Didier shook his hand, greeted Monique, and then gave Lilou a kiss on the cheek. She blushed as he took her by the hand and led her to the elevator. Riding down in close proximity to Didier made her heart flutter.

"I am so glad you agreed to see me tonight, Lilou," Didier said. "I thought tonight we'd go to Colline de Fourvière. There is a spectacular view of the city. And then we can go to a restaurant. I'd love for you to try real Lyonnaise food."

"Oh, yes." Lilou smiled. She'd heard about the famous Lyonnaise style of cooking from her mother, who had mentioned it when underscoring the superiority of the French way of life.

"Perfect, then we are off." He held the front door of the apartment building open for her. Lilou saw his car parked right outside. She thought of Cinderella, being swept away in a carriage.

Didier opened the passenger side door for her. As she sat down, the mini-skirt rode up, and she was conscious that he could see her whole leg. Lilou felt his eyes on her and trembled inside. *I am on my first date!* Lilou thought and felt jittery from excitement. They rode for a few minutes in complete silence.

"I am glad we met." Didier smiled, looking over at Lilou. He reached over and squeezed her hand. A current ran through her body at his touch.

Their conversation flowed easily over the next few hours. Didier told Lilou about his childhood, his siblings, the summers he spent in Bretagne with his grandparents. He did not mention his late wife until the very end of the evening.

"I suppose your aunt told you I've been married before," Didier said. They were driving back to the apartment, and Lilou was fully under the spell of the magical evening they had spent together.

"Yes, I am really sorry about what happened," she responded, trying her best to give her voice a reassuring tone. Lilou wanted to add "to your wife," but stopped herself. She bit her lip, suddenly incredibly sad for Didier and his past relationship. Lilou averted her eyes. When she looked up, he was looking at her intently.

"It's life." He sighed. "I learned a lot from the experience." Not knowing what to say next, Lilou nodded in response.

"I know it's just our first date, but I want you to know as much as possible about me and to learn what I can about you." Didier parked his car a few blocks from their destination. He looked at Lilou and took her by the hand. She turned to face him. A shadow from the streetlight fell across his face, so Didier appeared mysterious and regal.

"I like you," Lilou said, amazed at her own bravery.

"You do?" Didier's eyes sparkled, and he leaned in and kissed her. The kiss was long and passionate. *My first kiss,* Lilou thought as she melted in his arms. "Lilou," he breathed out.

They made plans to see each other the following evening. Lilou's visit to Lyon had a new purpose: spending as much time with him as possible. Her days were filled with anticipation of their evenings together, and at night she dreamed of Didier. By Thursday night, Lilou could hardly remember her life before their meeting. Gary was all but forgotten. Like an irrelevant, small, and useless part of her life.

I can't believe I was so silly. Lilou thought of how she barely got out of bed for over a month and would need to complete her junior year of college in September. Now, Lilou was with the person who mattered. A real date with a man she liked and who liked her back. The start of something with potential. Something real.

She knew it might all seem so impossible when she got back to Pittsburgh. But with her hands in his, and as he smiled at her warmly, she believed they could be together.

━━

"ARE you going to break up with that Marlboro man of yours?" Aline asked her. Her cousin sat on the bed, watching Lilou pack her suitcase for her departure.

"Umm, I don't know." Lilou bit her lip. *I can't explain to her that Gary isn't actually my boyfriend.*

"Didn't you and Didier make plans to see each other again?" Aline insisted.

"Listen, it's none of your business." Lilou frowned.

"I am just thinking, the spell that we did, it will work. So Gary might be very into you when you return," Aline said.

"So what?" Lilou brushed her cousin off. She shoved a shirt into the suitcase and slammed it shut.

———

THE FOLLOWING MORNING WAS A FRIDAY, and Didier had planned to open his office late so that he could see her off. He was waiting outside of her aunt's residence to pick her up early in the morning, his face somber. Lilou left the apartment quietly, having said her goodbyes the night before.

"I will miss you, Lilou. Please, when are you coming back to Lyon?" he asked as they neared the train station.

"Maybe next summer? I still have to finish college," she explained. "Just one more year."

"Oh, yes, that's right. I am glad that you are serious about your education." Didier nodded.

They did not discuss a future together in detail, and now it was as if there was a gaping hole, a void forming between them. *What will happen next?* Lilou thought, but immediately brushed her worry aside.

"Lilou, I'll think about how the two of us can be together," Didier said. "I will write to you."

"I'll write to you as well." Lilou breathed out. She leaned in to kiss him and as they embraced, tears welled up in her eyes. She did not want the fairy tale to end so quickly. Five beautiful days filled with love and joy with this man, and yet her whole life had turned around.

"Lilou, don't worry, we'll see each other soon. Maybe I can come to Pittsburgh next summer. We'll make it work." Didier gave her another kiss. It was time to board the train. So much had changed in her life since she first came to France. He waved at her, blowing her a kiss.

I will always remember this week as the best in my life, Lilou thought as she stared out the window.

Chapter 16
THE RETURN

Her grandparents were waiting for her at Gare de Lyon. As soon as Lilou stepped off the train, Grand-mère scanned her face and then clapped.

"Perfect! Our girl is in love!"

"Oh?" Her grandfather grunted and picked up the suitcase. "Let's go, I don't like where I left the car." He adjusted his cap and gave some passersby a firm stare.

"Bien sûr, Guillaume." Régine shook her head and then, turning back to Lilou, winked at her granddaughter. "Am I right?"

"Maybe." Lilou gave the woman a sly smile. Their interaction could not have been any more different from the greeting at the airport three weeks prior. She felt like a new person. There was a bounce in her step as she walked next to her grandmother, observing Guillaume's tall frame in front of them. They maneuvered through the train station and, despite the noise, Grand-mère managed to extract key information from her. Lilou had met a handsome doctor, they had gone on dates every evening in

Lyon, and they made promises to exchange letters and to see each other the following summer.

"Can't you stay longer, Lilou?" Régine offered. "Why don't you stay until the end of the summer, go back to Lyon, see him again?"

"My parents expect me back in Pittsburgh," Lilou countered. There was also the issue with her exams and the unfinished junior year of college, but she did not think her grand-mère would find that a legitimate excuse. *My parents must be worried about me,* Lilou thought. *They only sent me to France so I could get better, and now they want me back home.* "I don't think I can delay going back."

"Maybe we can think of something?" Régine suggested, her voice mischievous.

"Régine, please, let her be." Guillaume sighed, as he opened the trunk and placed the suitcase inside. Lilou immediately thought of their first encounter, and how large and impressive her grandfather looked at the airport. This time, he appeared tired, his shoulders slumped. His appearance contrasted with her grandmother's energetic figure. *I wonder what's happened,* Lilou thought as she climbed in the back of the car.

They pulled up to the cottage in Roissy in early afternoon. Lilou passed the rose bush in the garden, the one with which her grandmother spoke, and touched its petals. She felt as if it responded to her and noticed that its flowers looked fresher. *How wonderful,* Lilou thought. *I guess Grand-mère revived it after all.* She headed straight to the bedroom, which felt comfortable and familiar.

"Lilou, would you like to eat?" She heard her grandmother's voice coming from the kitchen.

"Yes, please," Lilou responded. As she walked in, she noticed a stack of letters on the kitchen table, and it hit her. *I need to write to Didier!*

"Grand-mère, is it okay if I write a letter?" Not waiting for an answer, she headed back to her bedroom, where her grandfather had already placed her suitcase. Lilou rushed to open it and pulled out a stack of postcards from Lyon. She chose the best one, with the view of the Colline de Fourvière and the beautiful basilica. It was the very place where Didier had taken her on their first evening out. Lilou stared at the picture with tenderness. *Just five days ago, but it seems like we've known each other forever.* The thought flashed through her mind. Lilou sat down to write, but soon realized that writing in French was difficult, more difficult than she expected. Struggling with almost every sentence, she resigned to using simpler words to ensure proper grammar. After several minutes, Lilou sighed, put down the pen and headed to the kitchen.

"What's wrong, chouchou," Régine asked. She stood stirring a pot, and a delicious smell permeated the room.

"I am just not sure. I have to write a letter. Didier and I agreed," Lilou sat back on a chair, "but my French, it's terrible. I can speak it, but writing is a whole different story."

"Oh, my poor dear." Grand-mère shook her head. "But don't worry so much, and you'll get better with time. It just takes practice. Maybe I can help you with the first few words?"

"Oh, yes, thank you!" Lilou perked up.

"Of course, after all, I feel partly responsible for this whole situation!" Grand-mère let out a giggle.

"What do you mean?" Lilou frowned.

"You are responsible, Régine!" Guillaume walked into the kitchen. His face bore a stern expression, and Lilou noticed wrinkles on his forehead.

"Oh, Guillaume, please." Régine raised her eyebrows

and opened the lid of the pot. Steam rose high above the stove.

"You should tell her, Régine." He sat down at the head of the table with a heavy sigh.

What's happening? Lilou scanned the faces of her grandparents for clues.

"Alright, alright." Régine placed the pot in the middle of the table. "I may have given you a love potion when you were here last week."

"What?" Lilou gulped. "A love potion?"

"You were so sad and downtrodden. I didn't know what to do. I was worried about you, and so I checked all my manuals. Love was the only thing that could cure you. So I gave you a love potion before you left for Lyon."

Lilou opened her eyes wide and stared at her grandmother. "So without the love potion, I wouldn't have met Didier?" Her mouth gaped open. The fairy tale meeting with Didier, their relationship, everything started to unravel.

"Oh no, it's not like that. You would have met Didier, but maybe feelings would have taken longer to develop. The potion sped up your romance, that's all. It's the cure you needed for your depression, my dear. I could tell you were suffering over a man, and Similia similibus curantur.[1]"

"What does that mean?"

"It means that you quickly needed a man in your life, and it worked out perfectly," Régine explained nonchalantly.

"Régine, you can't play God with your own granddaughter!" Guillaume sighed.

"I was just trying to help," Régine pointed to the set table. "Now, let's have a nice dinner together instead of arguing!"

Her grandmother spoke as if nothing extraordinary had happened. Lilou sat, her shoulders slumped and put down her fork, suddenly unable to eat.

"So what do I do now? Does this mean Didier doesn't really love me? I knew it was too good to be true." Tears streamed down her face. They fell on the postcard she'd been writing to him. Everything, the magical time she'd spent in Lyon, her relationship, promises of love, she did not deserve any of that. *I am a failure. I will be alone forever.*

"Oh, my dear, please, everything will be fine, you just have to give it time. Now you'll get to know Didier, you'll write letters, you'll build your relationship."

"But the potion?" Lilou whimpered. "You said there was a potion. And now, without it, Didier will go away?"

Régine gave her husband a side eye. "The potion only sped up things, like I said, but everything is real. Now you have a good man in your life, and things will just move along nicely."

"But it means he didn't actually choose me!" Lilou yelped.

Régine began serving stew next. "Of course he chose you!" She noted, putting a steaming plate in front of her granddaughter.

"But what will happen in the future?" Lilou remembered her cousin and her heart sank. *What if the spell I did with Aline interferes with my relationship with Didier?*

"No one knows that. And please don't worry about the love potion. I know what I am doing, Lilou. And I wouldn't do anything that hurts you or the other person. I have been practicing my craft for half a century! And it's not like it's a love spell! Now that's something I'd never do. Because a love spell forces the other person to develop feelings and compromises their free will." Her grandmother folded her arms. "A love potion I gave to you just made you more attractive to men, that's all."

"Régine, I have to say," Guillaume cleared his throat, "and I am not trying to interfere with your work, but maybe you should have told Lilou what you were doing first."

"Do you remember how she was acting when she first got here? What exactly was I supposed to do? And look how much better she is now! I don't understand why you are always trying to criticize my work."

"Alright, alright, at least you told her now." Her grandfather took a bite of the stew. "Thank you, Régine. The food is delicious." His tone was conciliatory, and Lilou had a feeling that her grandfather was afraid to contradict his wife. It was a familiar pattern. Lilou had seen the same between her parents, with her father rarely confronting her mother.

They ate in silence, Lilou mulling over the information she'd just learned. An uneasy feeling rose in the pit of her stomach, as she thought of Aline and the spell. Only then, she remembered Gary. *I should probably tell Grand-mère about the spell,* Lilou thought, as she finished eating. *But Aline doesn't want anyone to know, and she said her mother would be upset. Monique was so kind to me. I don't want them to have problems.* Lilou got up to help clear the table. *The spell probably isn't a big deal.* Lilou convinced herself and decided to not reveal information about it to her grandmother.

▭

TWO DAYS LATER, Lilou got comfortable on her flight back to Pittsburgh. Her trip to the airport and the day prior were uneventful. Other than writing a letter to Didier, she did little. The process of correcting her grammar and checking every word with her grandmother was incredibly tedious, so composing a one-page letter took hours. She'd planned on writing a letter on the plane, but now questioned her ability to write to Didier regularly over the course of the year.

As she sat on the plane, Lilou thought of the time she'd spent in France. She'd come to France broken and depressed, but found renewed hope for a brighter future. She had a love connection. A boyfriend of sorts. Maybe not quite a boyfriend, but a man who was interested in her and with whom she hoped to have a future together.

Lilou's parents greeted her at the airport. She noticed bags under her father's eyes as if he'd been having trouble sleeping. The expression on Katrine's face was impenetrable, but Lilou noticed that her mother scanned her face for clues.

"So, how was France?" Katrine kissed Lilou on the cheek.

"It was good," Lilou said and smiled, hoping that would reassure her parents.

"Linda, you look better!" Her father announced, giving her a hug. His words sounded like an affirmation.

"I feel better too." Lilou nodded and felt as if her parents let out a collective sigh.

As they drove home from the airport, Lilou kept up the conversation. She told her parents about her visit to Paris and then Lyon, how much she liked the city and how much she enjoyed the time spent with her aunt. She mentioned Aline in favorable light, telling her parents that her cousin was fun and sweet."

"And her husband? How was he?" Katrine asked, her eyes shifting.

"Oh, nothing much to say. He's a bit strange." Lilou responded.

"I see. And their apartment? It's nice?" Katrine turned back to face her daughter.

"It's nice, but small. But I liked Lyon, cute town. And they have a nice big park, right near where they live," Lilou added, pausing. She felt like a high-society gossipy woman and the feeling pleased her.

"Interesting, Monique never mentioned the park." Katrine shook her head and reached for a cigarette.

When Lilou was finally in her bedroom, she felt a strange emptiness. After several minutes sat on her bed, she rose and walked over to the window, trying to understand what was happening to her. She pulled back the curtain and stared at the house across the street. So much time watching Gary's house from her bedroom window, yearning for her neighbor. So many hours spent hoping to catch him outside, then reveling in their quick conversations. Since the first time they met, there wasn't one day when Lilou didn't think of the handsome guy next door. She'd been so fully dependent on him and his existence, on their future, but now she felt nothing.

Remembering Aline, Lilou thought that it would have been nice to have another girl around her age at home. As much as Aline had annoyed her, she had been a companion. *I wish Marianne would come back,* Lilou thought. With a sigh, she headed downstairs. Lilou hadn't exactly planned on telling her parents about Didier, at least not right away, but, as she was nearing the kitchen, she overheard her parents' conversation.

"Maybe someone will fall for Lilou," Katrine's voice sounded upbeat.

"I told you a long time ago, she just needs time," her father said. "Linda will show them!"

"In the end, I have to agree, Michael. Going to France had been a good idea," Katrine responded. There was a rustling sound, and Lilou could tell that her mother had just taken another cigarette out of a pack. "We should have sent her sooner. Maybe then we could have avoided that whole situation."

"Better late than never," Lilou's father responded. The clanking of cutlery followed.

Standing outside of the kitchen door, Lilou listened intently. Before going to France, she would have walked away, pained by her parents' discussion of her prospects. Her mother's judgment, her father's futile expressions of hope. But this time, things were different. Her parents thought she was getting better. They believed in her. Both of them. She could tell they cared about her. And she had proof of her recovery.

"I am so glad she went. She looks great, really!" Lilou could hear her mother puffing on the cigarette, then exhaling the smoke.

"Exactly."

Hearing her father's words, Lilou sucked in her breath and resolutely entered the kitchen, catching her parents by surprise.

"Maman, Daddy, I wanted to tell you, I met someone in France." Lilou cleared her throat. Her heart beat fast in her chest, she felt sweat forming on her forehead, but she stood still, watching her parents, savoring the stunned expressions on their faces.

"You did?" Her mother was the first to react. "A boy?"

"A man. He is a doctor in Lyon, his name is Didier."

"Oh, a doctor!" Katrine gave her daughter an approving smile.

"A doctor? Did he ever serve in the military?" Her father asked, narrowing his eyes.

"I am not sure." Lilou responded. "We spent time together and went on several dates over the week, and

Auntie Monique and her husband know him. He is friends with them."

"So he is what age, this guy?" Michael was still frowning, but the severe expression on his face eased somewhat.

"Late twenties. A widower," Lilou breathed out. Saying those words out loud was difficult, and 'widower' sounded as if Didier was guilty of surviving, but Lilou wanted to share the full picture with her parents.

"I see," Katrine nodded, seemingly unfazed by this information. "No kids, I hope?"

"No kids," Lilou added, feeling victorious.

"That's great, chouchou." Her mother was now smiling. "Do you have a photo of this doctor?"

"I do!" Lilou rushed out of the kitchen and ran upstairs. Didier had given her one photo of himself. He was standing next to his office, and the sign 'Cabinet Medical' was clearly visible behind him. Lilou thought the photo did not do him justice, but she was glad to have an image to show her parents. They were quiet as Lilou ran back into the kitchen, carrying the photo.

"Here," Lilou put it on the table and hovered, gripping the back of a chair in anticipation of her parents' reaction. Katrine looked at the image, nodding in approval. Lilou blushed with pleasure. Her father examined the photo next, frowned a little, and then gave Lilou a smile.

"He looks like a nice fellow," Michael Kelleher admitted.

"He is! He is very nice, and he said he has serious intentions!" Lilou repeated Didier's words. *Never-mind the love potion and whatever it took to find Didier.*

"He better!" Lilou's father said. "What is your plan now? Is he coming here to meet us?"

"Daddy, I don't know yet. We didn't agree on the details, but he said he will come up with a plan." Lilou tried to sound calm, despite feeling a slight feeling of unease about her future with the handsome doctor.

"It's okay, Lilou, you just met him." Katrine noted. "You have time."

"But Katrine, he's on another continent. Remember how it was for us?" Lilou's father turned to his wife.

"Michael, that was another time, right after the war. Things are different now." Katrine shrugged.

"Well, I suppose it is too early." Michael acquiesced.

"We've already started writing to each other! We will write every week, and maybe we can see each other next summer?" Lilou checked her parents' faces for clues.

"Maybe," they responded in unison. Her mother, having finished the pre-dinner cigarette, rose to heat up their food, and Lilou reached for the plates to set up the table.

Chapter 17
THE WEDDING

On the morning of Gary's wedding, Lilou felt calm and collected. She was dressed in a pretty yellow dress, her hair pulled back. Though Lilou never revealed the identity of her forlorn lover, she suspected that Katrine knew all along it was Gary. The worried expression on her mother's face as they got ready for the wedding confirmed her suspicions.

It was Saturday, August 11th, 1973. Her parents had received the invitation from the Blacklins, and they would attend Gary's wedding as a family. As the temperature reached almost 90F, Lilou wiped the sweat off her forehead.

"Lilou, did you put on your make-up?" She heard Katrine's voice as she headed down the stairs.

"I did." Lilou marveled at the fact that she was now being treated as a woman. She assumed that it was because of Didier, and the prospect of marriage to a French doctor, that their relationship had shifted. Love potion or not, Lilou felt like a different person, and she liked the new version of herself much more. She was happier.

"Lilou, please don't forget, I've got a few new clients. I'll get you their information later tonight."

A smile crossed Lilou's face as she heard Katrine's words. This had been another change in their relationship: her mother now volunteered information about Mary Kay sales and appreciated Lilou's help with accounting.

During the walk to the church, Lilou thought of her relationship with Didier. Almost two months had passed since they last saw each other, and they had already exchanged several letters. Just as she suspected, writing to Didier in French was a tedious process, but Lilou started to enjoy it. *And I am getting better at my written French grammar,* Lilou thought, pouring over yet another sheet of paper in which she recounted to Didier her daily activities. Writing about a summer in Pittsburgh, which seemed extremely boring to Lilou at first, turned out to be quite interesting.

Upon her return to the US, Lilou had pushed away the thoughts of the paranormal things that happened in France. The love potion, the spell, the strange dreams she had while visiting her grandmother, and even Régine's profession, all of those facts faded to the back of her mind. None of those things mattered. Instead, she focused on what she had to accomplish: graduating from college and keeping in touch with Didier.

Once inside the church, the Kellehers sat on the right side, in the back, along with other guests of the groom. They chit-chatted with their neighbors before the ceremony began. Gary entered the church, his slumped shoulders, like someone ill at ease. The black suit made him look like an undertaker. Lilou held her breath, waiting for the bride. She expected a beautiful, tall, fairy-like woman, but Sammy was short. So short that she looked like a little kid as she walked down the aisle. A veil covered the bride's face.

In a flash, Lilou remembered the horned creature in her dream on the flight to France and the torn veil. The memory pierced her and disappeared. Lilou strained her neck to get a better view of Gary's bride. The wedding dress exposed Samantha's shoulders, and Lilou could see her biceps even from the back of the church.

Lilou remembered little of the ceremony, but by the end she felt unnerved, despite telling herself that Gary no longer mattered to her. She fought the urge to leave right after, but something compelled her to stay for the reception. *I might as well, since I am here.*

The bride and groom walked out of the church. Sammy in front, while Gary followed a step behind. It looked as if the bride was leading her new husband. The bride's veil now pulled back, Sammy looked radiant. She had bright eyes and a small, snub nose. Her lips were thin, and she had a cleft chin.

The couple greeted guests one by one, and before she could get out of the way of the procession, it was Lilou's turn.

"Hi, congratulations!" Lilou squeezed out, feeling butterflies in her stomach. *It could have been me next to him*, she thought, watching Sammy. *But he'll see. I will marry a French doctor and move away from here. He'll understand what he lost.* She smiled at Gary and his bride.

"Thank you. Sammy, meet Linda. She is my neighbor. I told you about her." Gary blushed.

"Oh, yes, the one in college?" Sammy gave Lilou an assessing stare.

"Yeah, that's the one." Gary shrugged.

"Nice to meet you!" Sammy said, her voice perky. Lilou read menace in her rival's eyes.

"Nice to meet you, too!" Lilou responded, trying to sound gracious. "Congratulations on your big day!" The couple moved on, and Lilou thought that the interaction with the happy couple had gone smoothly.

Emboldened, she accompanied her parents to the reception. There, Lilou saw Gary's mother, but could not bring herself to say hello. She did not know most of the guests, and stood alone, watching her mother chat up potential clients. Lilou was about to leave, when Gary approached her.

"Hey, Linda, you've changed over the summer." Gary's face was flushed. He'd been drinking.

"Thank you. I came back from France a few weeks ago," Lilou responded, dignified. *This isn't so bad.*

"Groovy! You travel and you are smart!" Gary stared at her in admiration.

"Thank you," Lilou blushed. *Does Gary like me? But he is married now.* Lilou averted her eyes, trying to find an appropriate response. At that moment, Sammy walked up to them. She took Gary by the elbow and whispered something in his ear.

"Oh, sorry, we gotta go," Gary said, and a second later, he and Sammy disappeared into the crowd of guests.

On the way home that evening, Lilou's parents walked ahead, with her mother discussing the wedding and sharing how many new clients she would have thanks to the occasion.

Lilou's father listened silently and then noted, "That Gary is just like the rest of them. A deserter. Really, America is losing real men!"

"Michael, honey, that's not true. The draft is over now!"

"Funny how he spent five years at Penn State and came back without even graduating." Michael grumbled.

Lilou half-listened to her parents while absorbed in her own thoughts. *Does he love me? He told me I changed; he wanted me. But he is married now, this is terrible. What do I do? How do I behave?*

"I heard they are going to live in an apartment in Squirrel Hill. He's going to join the police." Lilou heard her mother say.

"I see. I guess that's better than mooching off his parents." Lilou's father sighed.

"I heard that Dorothy, Gary's mother, is not too happy with her new daughter-in-law."

"Katrine, these women are never happy!" Michael chuckled.

Gary should have chosen me, Lilou concluded. *His mother likes me. But it's too late now. I will marry Didier and Gary will be with Sammy.*

<hr>

Chapter 18
GARY

<hr>

May 1974

Graduation date was approaching. Four years of hard work about to pay off, and Lilou expected to graduate with a summa cum laude. The Kellehers spent weeks planning a graduation party. Katrine took the lead, encouraged by Lilou's plans after graduation. A potential marriage to a Frenchman, though a vague possibility, made her mother happy. It meant that her daughter would not end up alone, an old maid with a boring profession, but a French homemaker.

"My Lilou really is full of surprises," Katrine soon started telling her clients. "A hard worker, studies so much, really too much, but managed to meet a great guy." She would then take a drag on her cigarette and shrug. "I guess if it's meant to be, it's meant to be, and Lilou was always meant to live in France. I suspect she'll move there soon, once there is a proposal. But Michael and I wanted to make sure our daughter graduated first. Not to rush things."

Lilou overheard this speech several times, and it invariably made her cringe. She did not agree with this version of events. But Lilou never contradicted her mother, never pointed out that Katrine had always been against Lilou's degree in accounting, or anything to do with her academic achievements. For the first time in her life, Lilou had something she'd craved all along: her mother's approval.

Lilou savored the memory of the brief time she'd spent with Didier. How they held hands. The way Didier looked at her. The tender things he'd said to her. She knew that when they saw each other again, he would ask her to marry him. He'd hinted at the proposal in his letters, and she'd made the decision to postpone her job search until after her trip to France.

Though she did not discuss it with her parents, Lilou assumed she would go to France the summer after finishing college. She decided to ask her father for a ticket to France as a graduation present. Lilou counted the days until after the party was over. Studying for finals took so much energy that Lilou had little time left for anything else.

The idea of leaving Pittsburgh to live with Didier in Lyon made Lilou uneasy. *I guess I won't work in France,* Lilou thought, *or maybe Didier will move to America?* Lilou fantasized, but then immediately decided it would be difficult, given Didier's medical practice in Lyon. Through the letters so far, Lilou learned a lot about Didier's life. He wrote to her about his practice, and about how much he missed her. Didier's letters were filled with tenderness and love, and Lilou had grown used to reading and re-reading them daily.

The date of the graduation party was set. In preparation, Lilou went to get her hair and nails done. Her mother booked an appointment at a new salon in Shadyside. The owner was one of Katrine's Mary Kay clients and agreed to see Lilou as a favor. She'd never gotten a manicure before, and usually just got her hair trimmed. It was Lilou's first time doing something so adult and so glamorous. She walked into the salon, terrified, but also jittery with excitement. The hairdresser, a woman in her fifties, looked Lilou over and asked:

"What is it you'd like done today, hon? Maybe feathered hair, like that actress, Farrah Fawcett?"

"Is that possible? With my hair?" Lilou threw a skeptical look at herself in the mirror, examining her mousy locks.

"Of course, hun," the woman promised and set to work.

Two hours later, Lilou stared at her reflection. At a completely different version of herself. Her hair had been cut in beautiful layers and appeared to be at least twice as thick as before. Lilou now had a long set of acrylic nails that, according to the salon owner, were 'what they do in Hollywood these days." The nails felt uncomfortable, but she admired how uniform and long they looked.

The soft June wind ruffled up her hair, as Lilou walked down Walnut Street on her way home. She checked the time, and the sun reflected on the surface of her watch. It felt as if the whole world were smiling at her. She couldn't wait to show the new hairstyle to her mother. A bird chirped and Lilou looked up.

A crow perched on the branch of a pine tree. Opening its beak wide, the crow cackled and Lilou felt panic rise in the pit of her stomach. Pushing the unease away, Lilou hastened in the direction of her house. She was about to turn on to her street when she saw him. Walking towards her, hands in his pockets, whistling a tune.

"Hey, Linda! Long time!" Gary chuckled, and the sound reminded Lilou of the crow's cackle. Gary's face looked the same, the same wavy hair, blue eyes shining brightly. *I am over Gary! Why was I so into him before?*

"Hi, Gary," Lilou responded. She looked at him with wonder, trying to understand what had once attracted her to this completely unremarkable man.

"How you doing?"

"I graduated, finished my degree. We are having a graduation party soon," Lilou said, averting her eyes. "I think your parents were invited". She clearly remembered discussing with her parents whether to invite Gary and his new wife, and deciding against it.

"Graduation party! Lucky you!" A smirk appeared on Gary's face. "Umm, you wanna come over? See my new place? I rented an apartment nearby." He pointed to a high rise down the street.

"Did you guys move from Squirrel Hill?"

"No, Sammy and I..." Gary cleared his throat and looked at his feet. "Um, we separated."

"Oh, I am sorry," Lilou said, trying hard to sound compassionate.

"It's not a big deal," Gary shrugged. "So you are cool to come over?" Gary gave her a hopeful look. Lilou checked her watch. It was just after four. If she stopped by for a few minutes, she'd be home in time to help her mother cook dinner.

"Yes, I guess so," Lilou nodded. She was curious to see where he lived.

"It's right around the corner," Gary said and gestured for her to follow him down an alley. They walked to a five-story apartment building that Lilou had passed all of her life. She had never been inside. Gary opened the main door and entered the lobby first. Lilou followed him to the second floor. A few moments later, they stood in front of a shabby apartment door.

She noticed the number. 3F. She wondered why an apartment with that number was on the second floor. Gary unlocked the door and entered, not holding it for her. *I'll just stay for a few minutes and leave,* Lilou thought. She noticed a table with newspapers thrown on top, a dirty coffee cup, an ugly chair.

"Hey, you are cute," Gary said suddenly, turning to face her. "You know, Linda, I am sorry. I really feel like an idiot. I should have been with you. You're a real cutie, and you're smart."

"Thank you." Lilou stood in the middle of the living room, trying to understand if she should sit at the table or continue standing.

Gary approached, inching closer to her. "And how about you? You like me?" He was now inches away from her.

Lilou stepped back.

"A little bit?" he insisted.

Lilou took another step back until she was pressed against the wall. Gary stepped closer and squeezed her thigh.

"Do you?" He shoved himself against her. Lilou felt as if she was about to choke. Gary started kissing her neck, while his hands were moving under her dress, feeling her everywhere. Lilou clawed at him, pushing him away and let out a scream. She struggled to free herself.

Just as suddenly, Gary stopped and pulled back.

Oh, this isn't happening, she thought, unable to breathe. She felt as if she was about to float out of her body and leave it forever. That's when he kissed her on the mouth. His breath smelled of cigarettes and alcohol.

A cigarette appeared in his hands and he lit it. Lilou stood against the wall, unable to move. Her legs were shaking, and she felt she might collapse at any moment. *What happened?* A sickness rose inside of her.

"I need to go," she whispered. "I gotta be home," she clarified. Tears streamed down her face. Lilou moved to the door, but Gary blocked her way. He wrapped his arms around her and pulled her close.

"Where's the bathroom?" Lilou asked. He let her go and pointed to the back of the apartment. Lilou moved in that direction. She closed the door behind her and locked it. In the bathroom mirror, her eyes looked wild, her hair was ruffled. The toilet was filthy and a cigarette butt was floating in it. The sight made Lilou feel nauseous.

What have I done? Lilou thought. She looked at her nails and noticed that one of the acrylic nails had broken. *I must pretend like nothing happened.* Lilou decided. *I will just go home, take a shower, and I'll forget all about this.*

At that moment, she heard a knock. "You okay in there?" Gary asked.

"Yeah, just a second," Lilou responded, giving her voice a perky undertone. She took another look in the mirror, exhaled, and opened the door.

Gary was standing there. He took one look at her and pulled her to him.

"I want you so bad," he started to say, but this time, Lilou reacted quickly. She pushed him away.

"I can't, I gotta go," she mumbled then rushed out of the apartment, hearing the door slam shut behind her.

Once outside the apartment, Lilou dashed downstairs. She opened the front door, feeling the hot air on her face. She ran all the way home, fighting back angry tears. The vision of Gary, the dirty apartment, it was as if she'd just traveled to another dimension.

As if the grime and muck that she had read about, had seen in the movies, had somehow crawled and caught her, sucked her in and now she'd been tainted. She was no longer worthy of Didier. Not a bright college graduate who would travel to France and enjoy a carefree summer. Lilou felt like throwing up. She wanted to clean herself, to wash herself right away.

She opened the front door of her house and heard the familiar sound of clanking pots in the kitchen. *Maman must have started cooking,* Lilou guessed, and crept upstairs.

"How was the salon, Lilou?" She heard Katrine's voice calling.

Lilou yelled out, heading for the bathroom, "One second, will be right down!"

Once there, she stared at her reflection in the mirror. Her hair lay flat, the airy texture the stylist had achieved now gone. Lilou tugged at her tresses, trying to fluff the hair up, but could not replicate the volume from the salon.

She nearly gagged, remembering the dirty toilet at Gary's, the smell, his mouth on hers. A wave of nausea rose inside of her. *What do I do now?* Lilou checked her face. *I guess you can't really tell;* she thought, and then felt sick. *How did I walk home like this?* Lilou gasped, as she inspected her dress. The seam on the side had been torn. *Thank God none of the neighbors saw me on the way here.* Lilou turned on the shower. As she got in, she noticed a red mark on her thigh. *Where his hand gripped my leg,* she thought and swallowed in disgust.

"Lilou, what's taking you so long?" Her mother's voice reached her ears from downstairs.

"Coming!" Lilou yelled out. She stuffed the torn dress in the very back of the closet, and sat on her bed naked.

She pulled at her hair and then tugged harder and harder. *Why did I agree to follow him?* She pulled again. Pain shot through her head, and she wanted it to continue. She needed to be punished for what had happened. Lilou slapped the side of her head, and that made her feel better. She raised her head and then heard a noise in the corner of the room.

A mouse? Of course there would be a mouse! Lilou thought.

She jumped off the bed and went to the corner. The noise came from under an armchair, and Lilou looked under it. There was nothing, only an old sock. Lilou pulled it out and listened again. Nothing at first, but then she heard the same sound again, only this time it came from a different corner of the room, near the window. She rushed there and pulled back the curtain. Again, nothing. Lilou froze in place. *I am going to find you, and then I'll catch you,* she thought. *Stupid mouse, you think you can outsmart me?*

In front of her, in the darkest corner, she saw a pair of eyes staring. Eyes that did not belong to a mouse, unmistakably human. Lilou gulped and stepped back. She glanced away for a moment, and when she looked back, they were gone. A knot formed in her stomach and fear took over. *I am losing my mind.* Lilou thought. She sat on the bed and stared at the floor in front of her. The familiar feeling of desperation came over her. She was useless and needed to disappear.

"Lilou!" She heard her mother's voice and the next minute Katrine appeared on the threshold. "What's going on? Lilou?" Her mother looked at Lilou and opened her eyes wide. "What's wrong with your hair? Why aren't you dressed? You didn't like it?"

"Didn't like what?" Lilou fought back tears, as she started putting on her clothes.

"The haircut."

"Oh, no, I didn't. It looked strange." Lilou averted her eyes.

"And your nails? Show me. I want to see the famous

manicure." Katrine reached for Lilou's hand, and Lilou pulled back.

"Maman, I broke one of them. Sorry."

"You did? So you didn't like the salon? Not worth it?"

"I, I don't know, I guess I am not used to these places," Lilou mumbled.

"I knew it. I should have gone there with you! Are you coming to help me with dinner?" She paused. "Lilou, what happened?"

"I, I didn't like the salon." Tears streamed down her face. She had a horrible secret she could never share with anyone, especially not her mother. Deep shame penetrated Lilou's very being.

"Chouchou, it's nothing to cry over, just a haircut. Don't worry, we'll think of something for the party. Everything will be alright," Katrine said.

Her mother couldn't be more wrong. *Nothing would ever be alright.*

Chapter 19
THE GRADUATION PARTY

Following what she now called 'the incident with Gary', Lilou plunged into a dark depression. During the day, she barely managed to help her mother with party preparations, reviewing the RSVPs, acting the part of a soon-to-be graduate, while suppressing the feelings of despair. Nightmares haunted her. Her sleep became jagged and shallow. The minute she fell asleep, she relived the events in Gary's apartment over and over.

She would see his face, feel his body, feel a deep shame even in her sleep. *Why did I agree to go to his place? I could have said 'no'.* She took frequent showers, but they did little to help her feel clean. The feeling of being tainted forever, of dirt and filth, of having touched something so unclean and sleazy and of becoming a part of it possessed her.

She had been changed forever.

A new chapter of her life began, one with a questionable future. Her degree did not matter. Whatever relationship with Didier she had or could have had was shattered. She was not worthy of someone as pure as Didier, now that she was a tainted, disgusting creature who had been contaminated by Gary. Following 'the incident', she couldn't bring herself to write to Didier and abruptly stopped responding to his letters. The letters continued to arrive regularly at first, but then became less and less frequent, and eventually he stopped writing to Lilou altogether.

On the day of her graduation party, Lilou felt faint from the lack of sleep. The yellow dress her mother forced her to wear only accentuated the pallor of her skin. Lilou pulled at the fabric. Her mother blow-dried her hair and Lilou had her nails redone, but the hairdo felt ridiculous, as if she were a sad clown. That morning, Katrine helped Lilou do her make-up with the latest Mary Kay cosmetics.

"I think you want to go for a fresh look," Katrine said, as she applied nude eyeshadow on Lilou's eyelids." Katrine stepped back and frowned, as she checked her daughter's face.

Lilou had a flashback of sitting in Monique's boudoir, preparing for her first date with Didier.

"And a bit of rouge, just a tiny bit, you look so pale!"

"I don't feel well," Lilou added, her voice hoarse.

Lilou had initially decided to ask her parents to cancel the party right after 'the incident', but did not dare bring up the subject. But now, with her mother's remark, Lilou saw an opening. "Maman, I don't think I want the party," Lilou whispered.

"Lilou, don't be ridiculous!" Katrine shook her head. "Really? What an idea? The caterers are arriving soon. And we've invited Daddy's friends. Larry Coleman will be there."

"Larry Coleman? He wasn't one of the RSVPs." Lilou opened her eyes wide. She hadn't thought in months of her father's friend who had been her mentor. After her trip to

France, conversations about her job retreated into the background, and her father stopped mentioning Pedersen.

"Yes, of course, dear. Larry is very impressed by your achievements." Katrine shook her head.

"But the party, I don't feel good," Lilou pleaded.

Her mother's stern look said it all. A cancellation was out of the question.

THE GRADUATION GARDEN party at the Kellehers' attracted a diverse crowd. There were Michael Kelleher's colleagues. Katrine's clients who had become friends as well as friends who were now her clients. Notably absent were Lilou's classmates. As the only girl in her graduating class, she had shied away from socializing at college. At first, it was because of Gary. Lilou did not want him to be jealous of her. And once Gary got married, she was already a senior, and it was too late to become close to anyone else. After four years at Pitt, there was no one she wanted to invited to her party, despite her mother's encouragement to bring a friend. Lilou scanned the crowd of guests for Gary's parents, and breathed out in relief when she did not seem them.

"There she is!" She heard her father's voice. Lilou turned and saw her father standing next to Larry Coleman. Both men were holding bottles of beer in their hands.

"Linda, great to see you," Larry Coleman nodded in her direction. He rubbed his bald head and gave her a smile. "I hear you are graduating at the top of your class! Congratulations!"

"Thank you, Mr. Coleman." Lilou noted weakly and blushed, embarrassed by the reminder of her academic achievement. Especially since she viewed it as an extension of herself, it came to her as naturally as breathing.

"With honors!" Lilou's father gave her a proud look.

"So, Linda," Larry took a sip of his beer, "I was talking to your father, and I thought maybe you could come work for my firm. Pedersen Accountants is looking for talented people like you. I discussed with the other two partners at the firm, and we can take you on." The man gave her a serious stare.

"Thank you." Lilou's mouth gaped open as she heard Larry Coleman's words. His invitation to work at the top accounting firm was a surprise. Lilou had assumed she would need to search for work, apply, go through an interview process, and that it would all happen only some time in the future. The fact that she was a woman would likely prevent her from actually starting at a place like Pedersen Accountants. She thought it likely she would have to settle for a smaller firm.

"You just gotta come in for an interview next week, but it's more of a formality." Larry cleared his throat and looked at his friend.

"Thanks, Larry, I appreciate it." Michael patted his friend on the back.

"Yes, well, we are happy to take a chance on Linda here. I put in the word, all that, nothing to worry about. And we'll make sure she won't have to travel, none of those audits or anything," Larry looked directly at Lilou and she felt as if he could see right through her. As if he knew about what had happened to her, 'the incident.'

"Appreciate that, Larry. I know it wasn't easy for you, and with the travel and all that. She's a young woman, traveling with those men is definitely out of the question." Michael shook his head.

At the mention of men, Lilou felt a lump form in her

throat. She remembered Gary, his hands on her body. *Can Daddy tell?* She panicked, shifting her feet.

"I gotta say one thing, even without the audits, it's still a very demanding job, long hours, and you have to follow a dress code," Larry Coleman said, as he finished his beer.

"You hear that, Linda?" Her father fixed his eyes on her.

"Yes, Daddy." Lilou forced herself to look up at her father. "So, when would I start?" She heard herself say. Her voice sounded detached and professional, as if she were speaking about someone else.

"I negotiated July 1st." Larry set his drink on the table. "I hope that works alright for you."

"Oh, yes." Lilou nodded, once again able to disguise the fact that Larry's words caught her off-guard. July was several weeks away and yet it meant that she could not travel to France in the summer. "Thank you, Mr. Coleman," Lilou said and walked off to get some food. She was almost to the table, where the caterers had set the dishes, when she heard a voice.

"Hey, Linda."

Her back tensed, and she froze in place, refusing to believe it was him. Gary.

"Linda, congratulations!" A woman's voice said.

Lilou slowly turned around and saw Gary's mother. Mrs. Blacklin looked flushed, beads of sweat rolling down her forehead. "Hot day today! But I told Mr. Blacklin that I would not miss this party. And we brought Gary along. Of course, you guys are such good friends, after all." Mrs. Blacklin pushed her son forward. "Go on, Gary, say hello, don't be shy."

"Congratulations, Linda." Gary smirked as he looked at Lilou. "I heard you are top of your class."

"Thank you," Lilou mumbled. A lump formed in her throat.

"So, what are your plans for this summer?" Mrs. Blacklin asked.

"I am not sure yet." She wasn't about to share Larry's Coleman proposal with the Blacklins. "I hope to start working soon," she added.

"I see, that's splendid. Where will you be teaching?" Mrs. Blacklin gave her a curious look.

Lilou held her breath, desperately trying to stop herself from screaming. She felt nausea, as the events of her fateful encounter with Gary played over and over in her mind. She could smell his breath on her face, feel his fingers, his body pressing against her.

"I won't be teaching," Lilou forced a response. Her voice cracked.

"But you said you'll be working?" Mrs. Blacklin adjusted her glasses.

"I will work as an accountant." She felt as if Gary had changed shape and grown in size. A monster about to swallow her whole.

"Like those men? That's an idea!" Gary's mother widened her eyes. "Oh, here's Mr. Blacklin!" She turned and faced her husband. "Hear this, dear? Linda is going to work as an accountant."

"How interesting?" Gary's father frowned.

Lilou felt as if she were about to leave her body. Another moment and she would float away, rise above her own graduation party, fly away and disappear. That was the only answer to her suffering, to the pain she felt, the disgust and revulsion she experienced.

"Lilou, come here, please." Katrine appeared and pulled her daughter away. "I wanted to show the foundation you are wearing to a client."

"Maman, I need to go lie down," Lilou whispered. "I don't feel well."

"Please, pull yourself together. This party is for you!" Katrine hissed and pulled her along. "Jennifer, this is what I wanted to show you." Lilou saw a rail-thin woman in a red sundress, with tanned arms and feathered hair, just like in a fashion magazine. "I applied just a tiny bit on her cheeks, but you can barely tell. You see, it's the perfect color, isn't it?" Katrine pointed to Lilou's face. "You see, now, Lilou, please turn this way, so Jennifer can see, to the sun, voila, you see, it's this perfect shade of peach. You cannot tell she has any make-up on, can you?"

As usual, Katrine's French accent came in stronger when she was selling Mary Kay. Lilou suspected that her mother did that on purpose, so that there would be no doubt in her clients' minds that she had a European background.

"Lovely, I'll take it!" Jennifer said, peering into Lilou's face.

"And if you like, I've got a few other new items," Katrine whispered to Jennifer, her voice conspiratorial.

"Of course, of course. I appreciate it."

With Katrine now fully focused on her client, Lilou took advantage of the situation. She moved back, then took another step, and then, checking to make sure her mother was still absorbed in conversation, turned around and galloped to the house. She was almost to the door when she felt a tap on her shoulder. Lilou stopped and turned around. It was Gary, his expression solemn.

"Linda, I need to talk to you, please." He gulped.

Lilou felt the ground move under her feet. She tried to stabilize herself. Gary reached for her. She flinched, and the next second collapsed on the ground. The last thing she saw was a pair of eyes watching her. The same pair of eyes, the human eyes that she'd seen in her bedroom.

Lilou woke up on the couch in the living room. The soft afternoon light was streaming through the windows. She heard voices in the garden. *The party still hasn't ended,* Lilou thought dejectedly. She touched her head and felt a wet napkin pressing down on her forehead. She took a deep breath and felt tears well up in her eyes. She heard her parents' hushed voices coming from the kitchen.

"How did you let this happen? Did you know she wasn't feeling well?" Her father's voice sounded accusatory. Lilou removed the wet cloth and sat up.

"I thought she was exaggerating. You know how Lilou is." Katrine defended herself. There was the clinking of glasses. "Anything to get out of socializing."

"Katrine, this could end badly. She is so fragile."

Lilou rose from the couch and crept to the kitchen, hiding behind the wall. There, she froze in place, listening intently.

"We invited all your friends, all your colleagues, Larry Coleman! We couldn't cancel it." Her mother insisted.

"Katrine, what if the same thing happens?" Michael cleared his throat.

He means how I was before I went to France, Lilou felt a lump form in her throat. *My parents think I am crazy.* Tears began streaming down her face.

"She'll be fine, things are different now," Katrine said, her voice now louder. Lilou heard a lighter going off, and the smell of cigarette smoke followed.

"But we can't keep sending her to France every time she has a breakdown! Besides, Larry offered her a job. She starts in July," her father said.

"What about that nice doctor?"

"Katrine, Linda needs a future. Going to France over

the summer to see some guy she barely knows is not what will get her far in life. You saw for yourself, she's still so weak. We should have been more careful with her."

Lilou sniffled upon hearing her father's words. Her father was right. She couldn't go to France, but for a different reason.

"My sister vouched for him!" Her mother's voice sounded shrill.

"So why did Linda spend the last four years studying accounting? Is it to move to France to be with some guy who hasn't even proposed yet?"

"He'll propose this summer. We have to give him a chance!"

"Why doesn't this guy come to Pittsburgh? If he wants to see Linda, he can come visit us here. If he is serious about her." A chair scraped on the kitchen floor. Then her father sighed. Lilou knew he must have sat down in his favorite spot by the window.

"His medical practice. He can't leave it!"

"Listen, Katrine, the way I look at it, if a man wants a woman, he'll go after her. Not the other way around. Our Linda deserves better."

I deserve nothing, Lilou thought. She crept back into the living room and sat on the edge of the couch. *Why did I go to Gary's apartment? What was I even thinking? It's all my fault. I am a dirty whore and I ruined my life.* She was carried away to her encounter with Gary in his apartment, tracing her steps, trying to pinpoint the time where she went wrong. *It must have been the way I smiled at him. I shouldn't have done that.* She heard laughter coming from the garden. Lilou turned and listened and then rose from the couch and headed upstairs to her bedroom. Once in the safety of her room, she shut the door.

And then she heard it. The squeaking noise. Just like a

mouse, as if it was scuttling under her bed. *I am going to catch you!* Lilou kneeled and looked under the bed. The space under her bed was empty, only a forgotten scrunchy lay in the corner. Lilou reached for it and suddenly felt something touch her fingers. She yelped and jerked her hand back.

The touch was not furry, like she would have expected a mouse to feel, but felt like skin. *Human skin.* She peered under the bed again, and this time she saw them. The pair of eyes staring back at her. She recognized them right away. She had seen them before.

Forgetting all about her party and Gary, Lilou laid flat under the bed and reached as far as she could with her hand.

"Hey! What are you?" she whispered to the creature. "What do you want?" She heard a squeak, and then – silence. Lilou pushed her body forward and craned her neck. The eyes were no longer there. She moved her hand forward, trying to reach as far back as possible. And there it was again, the soft touch of a tiny hand.

"Ahh!" Lilou yelled and pushed herself from under the bed. She stood up and examined herself. Her yellow dress now covered in dust.

"Lilou! There you are! Are you alright?" Her mother walked into her bedroom.

"Linda, we were worried about you!" Her father was right behind his wife. "What's going on? What are you doing?"

"I, I think I saw a mouse, something strange, under the bed. I heard a noise," Lilou responded.

Her parents exchanged glances. "Umm, listen, sweetheart…" her father started, then, looking at his wife, fell silent.

"Lilou, your father and I, we think that the idea of

traveling to France this summer might not be a great one."
Katrine cleared her throat. "We think that it's best that you
start working, just as Larry Coleman suggested."

"Yes, Lilou, the start date is soon, and you are not
feeling well. That's clear now, so it's too risky. It's important
that you get that job, get settled, and then we'll see. Alright,
sweetheart?" Her father's tone was ingratiating.

"Yes, Daddy." Lilou nodded, glad that she hadn't raised
the possibility of going to France before the party. She fully
agreed with her parents: going to France was not a good
idea. *Didier would never want to be with me now. He will know,*
she thought.

"So it's settled then, July 1st you start at Pedersen
Accountants."

"Yes, Daddy."

"Are you feeling better, Lilou?" Her mother narrowed
her eyes. "What happened to your dress?"

"I, I was checking under the bed. For the mouse."

"So you are well enough to search for a mouse? Let's
go back to the guests, Lilou. I think you've taken enough of
a break." Katrine shook her head. "Unbelievable."

"But maybe I should stay inside. I, I still don't feel
good."

Her mother grabbed her by the hand and dragged her
downstairs. "That's enough, Lilou, let's fix your dress, and
please go speak to the guests. It's your party."

Chapter 20
PEDERSEN ACCOUNTANTS

Lilou spent the summer of 1974 adjusting to Pedersen. The new job left her little time for rumination, which she was grateful for. She dedicated herself to proving that she was worthy of working at one of the top accounting firms in the country. She couldn't let Larry Coleman or her father down. The idea of traveling to France and being with Didier receded into the background.

She was the youngest employee and the only woman accountant at the firm. All others were middle-aged men, whose conversations focused on sports and the unreasonable demands of their wives. Lilou was assigned to work with an experienced Senior Accountant, Mr. Bradford. He was a lean, tall man with a glistening bold head.

On her first week in the office, Mr. Bradford dumped a folder, bursting with papers, on her desk and requested it to be 'organized and reviewed' by the time he got back from a two-week vacation. Lilou was apprehensive at first, but the task was much less complicated than doing the books for her mother's Mary Kay business, and Lilou finished it in less than a day. The rest of the time, Lilou spent reading

Pedersen Accountants manuals. When Mr. Bradford examined the documentation upon his return, he stared at the neatly presented information.

"You did this?"

"Yes." Lilou blushed.

"Excellent," Mr. Bradford concluded. He began assigning Lilou more and more work. The man traveled regularly for audits, and soon he was relying on Lilou for all his documentation. Ahead of each trip, he would come and ask her to review the documents. Lilou obliged. When she noticed that he rarely left the office without taking work home with him, Lilou started doing the same. At home, she peered over paperwork and her workdays were regularly over twelve hours long.

"Lilou, this is too much," her father would say, seeing her stare at yet another pile of papers after dinner.

"But Daddy, this is just like reading those math books, only now I get paid for it." Lilou would smile at him. She loved her job. She loved being around numbers, loved reviewing information, putting numbers together, like pieces of a puzzle. There was logic and safety in them. They made sense. They could be trusted. Unlike people. Unlike men. Unlike Gary.

Slowly, her memory of that terrible afternoon receded. She was barely at home and never walked anywhere near Gary's apartment. Lilou made sure to never go to Walnut Street alone. She worked long hours in the office, came home to eat and sleep, and often worked from home. On weekends, she told her parents she was too tired to leave the house.

This is perfect. I never have to see Gary or anyone else! That was the only way Lilou felt safe.

She got up at five thirty and left the house a little after six. *I am perfectly fine,* she thought while getting ready for work in the darkness. Lilou started eating breakfast in the office, because it helped her avoid her parents. She ate her cereal quietly at her desk, while staring at yet another set of papers. Lilou loved being productive. She was first to arrive in the office and last to leave.

Her zeal did not go unnoticed. A little over two years after joining Pedersen Accountants, she received a promotion. It was the day before Thanksgiving break, 1976, and all Pedersen staff assembled in a meeting room.

"Well done, Linda!" Larry Coleman shook her hand. "You've earned this'!"

"I am proud of you, Linda," Mr. Bradford added.

"Thank you, Mr. Coleman, Mr. Bradford." Lilou smiled at her mentors. Surrounded by her colleagues, she was standing in the meeting room that she'd gotten to know so well. The familiar walls that she'd seen in all hours of the day comforted her. She belonged at Pedersen. These men who worked tirelessly, who traveled, who audited, were after the truth, just like she was. It was their joint quest for balance. They needed to even out the numbers and make everything add up. Lilou loved speaking the same language as them, loved understanding what they were saying, loved the certainty of their profession.

There was one big difference between Lilou and those men: they had their own families outside of the office. Wives, children, in-laws, cookouts, picnics, and family vacations. They had 'problem children', wives who complained about their travel and work schedules, mysterious family obligations, and *dinners*.

"I gotta be home for dinner," they said as they left the office, inevitably carrying a briefcase bursting with paperwork. "Will review and have it ready in the morning."

Unlike her colleagues, Lilou did not have to be home for dinner. Her parents were used to her late arrivals and ate dinner without her. If she came back after seven, she expected the empty kitchen and to find her parents watching TV in the living room. Lilou simply re-heated the food and ate alone, flipping through papers in silence.

The thought of one day getting married made Lilou cringe. She sometimes remembered Gary and immediately froze inside. And then she would think of Didier, their romantic walks, how they held hands, and sadness overcame her. Her eyes filled with tears and she forgot her successful career, achievements, and high salary for a moment.

I am not cut out for a relationship, Lilou thought in those darker moments. *I am just pathetic. Who would want me now?* And if my mother knew the truth. She pictured the judgmental glances Katrine would give her. Once Lilou started working at Pedersen, Katrine had stopped trying to improve her daughter and no longer mentioned Didier. The memory of her trip to France long faded. Once or twice, Lilou thought of writing to Grand-mère, but could not bring herself to do it. She was simply too busy at work.

After receiving news of her promotion, Lilou came home in high spirits, eager to tell her parents. She opened the front door and heard loud voices coming from the kitchen. She set her briefcase on the doorstep and listened. Lilou did not like surprises. Katrine rarely brought clients over in the evening. Most of the Mary Kay business took place mid-morning, when husbands were at work and children were at school.

Maybe Daddy has a friend over? Lilou hung up her jacket, trying to stay as quiet as possible. Normally, in a situation like this, she headed straight to her room and hid until things quieted down. She even had crackers and chips in her room just for that reason – so that she could avoid socializing.

But something pulled her toward the kitchen.

Lilou stopped right outside the door. There was the sound of voices, the clanking of dishes, as if her parents were hosting a party. *Did I forget they were having company tonight?* she thought and then she heard the voice she would recognize anywhere. *Marianne!*

Her mouth gaped open, as Lilou walked into the kitchen, and took in the normally pristine kitchen table that was bursting with dishes, and noticed that her mother's favorite china was out. Sitting next to her parents was Marianne. Her sister looked different from the girl who had left home nearly ten years prior. Marianne's hair was long, her face looked tanned, but the smile was the same. Kind and bright. And her eyes, her blue eyes were unchanged.

"Marianne?" Lilou said and felt tears well up in her eyes.

"Lilou!" Marianne jumped up and hugged her. "Finally! You are home! I've been waiting for you." Marianne smelled like sandalwood incense.

"You're back!" Lilou scanned her sister's face.

"I am here for Thanksgiving! Visiting for a few days. I am going back to Cali in mid-December, taking the bus." Marianne took a step back. "Let me look at you!" She stared at Lilou. "A suit! You wear an actual suit!"

"We have a strict dress code in the office," Lilou said, feeling her cheeks flush, noticing the stark contrast between their appearances. Lilou was dressed in a dark brown suit she'd gotten at Talbots. Like the rest of her life, the clothes she wore to work were part of a well-planned routine. She owned several suits, all in dark colors, wore them with different shirts, either white or off-white. Lilou felt her legs, covered in pantyhose, chafe.

Marianne wore a long, flowing velvet skirt and a fluffy

sweater. The sleeves of her sweater looked ragged, with thread sticking out, but its blue color matched Marianne's eyes perfectly.

"I hear you are an accountant!" Marianne smiled. "That's groovy!"

"Yes." Lilou gave a dignified nod. She was unsure how to speak to her sister, and looked at her parents, searching for clues. Her mother reached for a cigarette, her eyes red, as if she had recently cried. Her father drummed his fingers on the table, his forehead creased. "So, what are you doing out in California? Are you living in a commune?" Lilou tried to keep the conversation going.

"I work at a farm. An organic farm. Didn't you tell her anything?" Marianne frowned and stared at her parents. In response, Katrine shrugged.

"You've been in touch?" Lilou stepped closer to the table and folded her arms. Her parents were silent, and that was her answer. "I don't understand. Why didn't you say anything?"

"Not exactly in touch, Lilou. Please don't fret. It's just that we were worried about you, your father and I, and so we contacted Marianne before you went to France. But then…" Katrine turned to her husband for support, and Michael obliged.

"Linda, you know, with everything that was happening to you, we were concerned. Marianne's life was not exactly the most stable."

"But you pretended like she didn't exist! For years! Why?" Lilou's heart beat so fast, she felt as if she was going to collapse. She could not remember the last time her parents had mentioned Marianne, and she never brought up her sister, thinking the topic would upset her parents. It was as if Marianne had disappeared without a trace, as if she'd never existed at all, but now it turned out that only Lilou had been kept in the dark.

"Linda, please control your temper. Your mother and I were concerned. We thought it was for the best. We tried to protect you!"

"Protect me from what? I am fine!" Lilou screamed in indignation, a sudden rage fueling her whole being. She clenched her fists and wanted to punch the table, break the plates, scream and shout for the whole world to hear.

"You are fine now, but not a few years ago, when you were going through your crisis." Her mother raised her eyebrows.

"I've never had a crisis!"

"Lilou, please, quiet down, maybe it's not the right word," Katrine started, but Michael put his hand over hers and she paused.

"Linda, your mother and I were afraid that you would run away. To find your sister. You seemed unstable. That's all."

"And now? I am not unstable anymore?" Linda leaned against the kitchen cabinet, suddenly feeling weak. She'd been living in a bubble that her parents had created to keep her isolated from the world and missed out on a real connection with her sister. "So you were lying to me all this time?"

"We weren't lying. We were just not sure you were ready for the truth."

"I am sorry, Lilou." Marianne rushed to hug her sister. "I should have insisted. They wouldn't let me write to you. Or call."

"I, I just don't understand!" Lilou yelled. She watched her mother, father, and Marianne, their faces merging into one. *They still think of me as a child.* Lilou stumbled back, pulling away from the grasp of her family. Lilou rushed out of the kitchen and ran to the front door. *I need to get away!* She hastily grabbed her jacket and bolted out of the house.

"Lilou! Wait!" Marianne ran after her. "Please, I am sorry."

"Leave me alone." Lilou yelled and ran onto the street. The cold November air burned her lungs. Her work pumps were not made for the frigid weather and her feet were soon freezing. She ran, not caring where she was going. After several blocks, her breath caught and she slowed down.

"Lilou!" Marianne grabbed Lilou's hand. "Please, please, stop. I am sorry this happened. I am sorry. They wouldn't let me talk to you. It wasn't my idea. And I had no clue about what you went through. They only told me you were doing well and that you went to college. That was it."

"Marianne, I missed you so much!" Lilou burst out crying. "I was so alone. I was all alone with them."

"My poor sis, I love you." Marianne hugged her tightly. "I am back, at least for a few days. We'll spend time together, okay?"

"Can't you stay?" Lilou begged.

"I am sorry. I have to go back to the farm. I can't leave, I run it. With Frank."

"Who's Frank?"

"My partner. Listen, let's go back, it's freezing." Marianne shivered and tugged at the sleeves of her sweater to cover her hands.

"I am sorry, I just…" Lilou sniffled. "I just didn't know what to do."

"I know, I know. Maman can be so cruel, that's why I ran away in the first place."

"I wish I could run away, too." Lilou looked at her sister.

"Maybe you can just move out of the house?" Marianne suggested.

"Maybe." Lilou said, swallowing hard. The truth of the matter was that despite her salary, Lilou was afraid to live alone.

The sisters walked back side by side, chatting. As if the years of separation had never happened. Marianne held Lilou's hand, and Lilou felt like she had when she was a little girl, admiring her older sister who was wise and beautiful.

"How did you learn to run so fast?" Marianne giggled as they neared the house.

"I think I was just really angry," Lilou responded and felt new tears well up in her eyes.

"Maybe you can come and visit me on my farm? It's beautiful out there. And we have a lot to do! You can come and live with me if you want."

They entered the house and Lilou lowered her voice. "I can't, my job, Marianne." A carefree vacation in California did not align with Pedersen Accountants standards in Lilou's mind. She tried to picture putting in a leave request, and the first thing that came to mind was Larry Coleman's disappointed face. "But we counted on you, Linda," she pictured him saying. And then Mr. Bradford appeared, pointing to a huge stack of papers.

"I am absolutely frozen!" Marianne shuddered as she walked in. Lilou closed the front door behind them.

Their parents sat in the living room, watching their two daughters in silence. Katrine was smoking a cigarette, while a lit one burned in the ashtray. Their father was next to their mother and wore a look of concern.

"Linda, we need to talk, I have to say," Michael Kelleher rose and took a hesitant step toward the sisters. "I, we, I am sorry. We tried to do our best." He averted his eyes. "And your mother, she, she wants to say something, too." She looked over to her daughters, but said nothing. "Katrine?" Michael urged. His wife puffed on the cigarette.

"I don't know. We did the best we could!" Katrine finally announced. She then rose, shook the ash off the cigarette, put out the other lit one, and headed to the kitchen. Lilou thought she heard her mother mutter, 'Incroyable'[1], as she closed the kitchen door behind her.

Chapter 21
THE OUTING

"Daddy, Lilou and I are going out," Marianne announced, as soon as their mother disappeared from view.

"Where?" Michael and Lilou asked in unison.

"You guys are funny!" Marianne smiled. "We'll just go out on Walnut Street. I was out there earlier. There are all those bars, new ones, too."

"You were out?" Lilou opened her eyes wide.

"Yes, I got in this morning. I took a walk while waiting for you to come home. Walnut Street looks amazing! I heard there is a great music scene, too!"

"I guess," Lilou shrugged, feeling a slight pang of unease. She'd paid little attention to entertainment events happening in their neighborhood, Shadyside, or even the entire city of Pittsburgh. There was no reason to go anywhere.

"Let's go to one of the jazz clubs! I am just going to put something sparkly on." Marianne's face lit up with a smile, and Lilou nodded in response.

I can't say 'no' to her, Lilou decided and, without wasting a moment, headed to her room. "Alright, I'll change. Give me a second," she yelled. Once in her bedroom, Lilou rummaged in her closet. *What do I wear?* She looked over the row of suits hanging in a neat row, their dark hues staring back at her in judgment. On the other side of the closet hung the button-down shirts. White, off-white, beige. Her weekend clothes consisted of jeans and t-shirts, and a few sweaters for the winters.

Lilou searched for something that would be appropriate for a night out, a low-cut shirt, a skirt that exposed her legs, but there was nothing. She remembered the outfit she'd worn on her first date with Didier, the last time she'd worn a mini-skirt. Lilou reached in the very back of the closet and noticed something.

For a moment, Lilou's heart leaped in anticipation of a long-forgotten, cute item of clothing that would make everything better. She reached for it and pulled out a crumpled dress. It was wrinkled and torn.

The very dress she wore when 'the incident' with Gary happened.

Lilou's head started spinning. She sat on the bed and gripped the cover. Her knuckles turned white. *There is no point,* she thought. *It's all useless anyway, and going out with Marianne is a stupid idea.* There was a knock on the door.

"Hey, are you alright in there?" Marianne walked into her room. She was already dressed in a pair of jeans and a cute, shimmery top.

"Marianne, I have nothing to wear." Lilou sighed. "I am not going."

"I knew it. Here!" Marianne produced another shimmery top. It was light-green, a beautiful shade that went well with Lilou's complexion.

"Thank you!" Lilou exclaimed and reached for it, her hesitation gone. Marianne's good mood felt infectious. The top fit Lilou perfectly. "Is it okay with these?" She pulled on a pair of jeans and spun in front of the mirror.

"Yes! Love it!" Marianne squeezed her in a hug.

"Do I need to put on make-up?" Lilou stared at her sister, wide-eyed, suddenly remembering that going out didn't mean simply getting dressed.

"I forgot all about Maman's obsession. Remember, I'd left before the Mary Kay craze," Marianne giggled. Lilou stifled a laugh.

"Let's put some on anyway, I have a whole stash right here." Lilou pointed to her bathroom, where cases of Mary Kay make-up her mother had given her during her senior year of college sat, mostly unopened.

"MAMAN, Daddy, we'll be back in an hour," Marianne announced. "Come on, let's run." Marianne pulled her along, they rushed outside and dashed toward Walnut Street. It was the second time in less than an hour that Lilou ran on the dark streets of Shadyside, but this time her mood couldn't be more different. She wasn't running away, she was heading towards something. She felt like she belonged, someone cared about her. Marianne was next to her, and they held hands. The two of them didn't speak until they approached the storefronts on Walnut Street.

"Which one do you want to go to?" Marianne paused, catching her breath.

"How about right here? Is that a club?" Lilou pointed to a door that read 'Casbah'. They could hear the sounds of jazz emanating from inside.

"Sounds like it," Marianne said and pulled open the door. There was a bar in the back and Marianne pulled Lilou there. "Here, let's sit right here." She pointed to a bar stool and smiled at the bartender. Lilou stood next to her sister, not sure what to do. "Sit down, Lilou. Let's have a drink." Marianne patted her gently on the shoulder.

Lilou nodded and sat on a stool. A knot formed in her stomach as she looked around the dimly lit space. *I am going to see him tonight,* Lilou thought. It was an intuitive feeling, an understanding. Fear of seeing Gary was the reason she had been living as a hermit for the last two years, and only left her house to go to Pedersen Accountants. But with Marianne's arrival, Lilou felt that her life was about to shift. The feeling unnerved her.

"What's wrong, Lilou? Is it your first time at a bar or something?" Marianne asked and gave her a concerned look. "Here, I got you a beer." A glass magically appeared in front of them, and Marianne pushed it towards Lilou.

"Thank you." Lilou took a sip and cringed at the sour taste. The cold glass sent shivers down her spine.

"I'm glad we got to see each other." Marianne had drunk a good half of her glass and winked at Lilou.

"Me too." Lilou nodded. "So, a farm?"

"I keep forgetting that our parents have told you nothing about me." Marianne adjusted her hair and shook her head. A man appeared next to them and leaned on the bar, closing in on Marianne.

"Hey there, ladies, home for the holidays?" He crooned.

"I am." Marianne fluttered her eyelashes at the man. Lilou stared straight forward, waiting for her sister to stop speaking, trying to be invisible. The man felt like an intruder.

"And your friend?" The man turned at Lilou and gave her an approving stare.

"Actually, that's my sister. She is a Pittsburgh girl." Marianne giggled.

"Sister! Wow! You two are some serious cuties!"

"Thank you," Marianne responded. Lilou stayed silent.

"I'm Jerry, by the way," the man extended his hand. "I got a friend, we are sitting over there," he pointed to a table in the back, "you two wanna join us?"

"Thank you, not right now," Marianne answered with firmness in her voice. Lilou continued staring at her glass of beer. "Maybe in a little while. We gotta do some catching up." She nodded at her sister. Lilou expected the man to take offense, to complain or protest, but he simply disappeared.

How does she do that? Lilou wondered.

"So, where were we?" Marianne shifted in her seat and moved slightly closer to Lilou.

"We were talking about how our parents hid the truth." A rueful smile crossed Lilou's face.

"I know. I am sorry, it's my fault, too," Marianne sighed. "I should have insisted, or come home sooner, but it was just too much, you know?"

"What was?"

"Everything. I ran away with Patrick, remember? It was amazing at first. We were in love, we joined this commune in California. Patrick knew some people there. He'd met them in Pittsburgh. It was the most beautiful time."

"Yeah," Lilou nodded. She remembered that time differently. Marianne's note. Her parents' stunned faces. Their house was filled with smoke with her mother going through two packs of cigarettes a day. Their father, angry at first, then quiet and brooding, with rare angry explosions of emotion directed at draft dodgers.

"We stayed at the commune for a few months. Maybe even a year. I don't remember it too well, because one day

Patrick just left." Marianne said, oblivious to Lilou's thoughts.

"What do you mean, left?" Lilou shifted in her seat. She'd expected a story of continued bliss from Marianne.

"He left, that's all. He took everything with him, left in the middle of the night. I knew right away he went to Canada. Because of the draft. He'd told me he was afraid of being found, of being sent to Vietnam. Our commune was pretty visible. Patrick worried there would be a raid. But I never knew he had plans to run away. He never mentioned it to me." Marianne shrugged. "Maybe it was my fault, but I was young. Twenty! What did I know?"

"Of course," Lilou nodded, trying hard to understand her sister's relationship with her ex. *Twenty.* The age that Lilou expected would make her life better, but instead, everything went awry. Lilou felt a knot form in her stomach. *Gary.*

"But that's how I ended up alone. A bit later, I learned he didn't leave by himself, but with another woman. There was this chick, a complete idiot, from Texas. She was from a rich family, gorgeous, and fell for Patrick, real hard. So the two of them disappeared together. I was devastated. Cried so hard, even thought of returning home."

"You did?" Lilou looked up at her sister, trying to imagine what would have happened had Marianne returned home in 1970 instead.

"Yeah, I did, I wrote to Maman, waited and waited, no response came. So I figured I was on my own, and I did it to myself. It was my choice, right? No way back." Marianne finished her beer and gestured at the bartender. A second glass appeared in front of her instantly.

"But then what? How did you end up on a farm?"

"Yes. The farm. In our commune we grew vegetables, all of that, but it wasn't big, not commercial or anything.

But at some point, I figured I had a real talent for this kind of stuff. Like it came easily to me. The flowers I planted bloomed real nice, the seeds would take, and I just enjoyed it, you know." Marianne looked at her hands, rough with chipped nails.

Lilou nodded, thinking about Régine and her beautiful garden.

"Yeah, and then, well, there was this guy at the commune, but he left shortly after I got there. And then he came back for me. Asked me to join him – he'd bought a farm. And he asked me to come live with him, work on the farm. So that's my story." Marianne smiled brightly.

"And that was Frank?"

"Yes. He's real nice. We are good together. The farm is hard work, but I love it. This time of year is the only time I can leave it. The rest of the year is super busy. Planting. The harvest. Sales. Maybe you can come out there, meet Frank, see everything for yourself?"

"Maybe," Lilou nodded. She pictured her sister's life, idyllic, with a tall, handsome Frank by her side, surrounded by the lush greenery of California farmland. "Do you grow peaches there? Oranges?"

"We do," Marianne giggled. "Aren't you going to finish your beer?"

"No, I think I am good," Lilou responded, averting her eyes. Marianne was brave and strong, so unlike her. *Why can't I be like Marianne? We are sisters, aren't we supposed to be alike?*

"Let's head out." Marianne pulled at Lilou's sleeve, and this gesture, so familiar, so friendly and caring, made her feel even worse. Tears flooded her eyes. "Lilou, what's wrong, honey?"

Lilou burst into tears. She wasn't holding them back anymore. Marianne did not say a word. She pulled Lilou into a hug, squeezing her tightly. "I am sorry. I'm sorry things turned out this way. Let's walk home now, okay? I should have known. We should have just taken it easy tonight. It's too much of a shock."

"No," Lilou squeezed out. She looked up at Marianne, knowing that tears must have made her face look red and swollen. Lilou could not remember the last time she cried like this, and the release of hot tears felt good. She noticed the bartender give them a curious look, but he spun around, trained to mind his own business.

"Are you okay to walk back?" Marianne nudged at her, once the tears receded. Lilou nodded and, leaning on her sister, headed to the exit.

"Hey, ladies, Jerry here, thought I'd, umm," the man who'd hit on them at the bar approached, but then, seeing Lilou's face, stopped short.

"Jerry, it was nice meeting you," Marianne said with a smile. Lilou wondered how her sister maintained appearances, regardless of the circumstances.

"Thought I'd give you my number, just in case, your sister, well, if she's interested," Jerry said, as he handed Marianne a piece of paper. He then turned and walked away from them briskly.

As tempting as it was, she pushed away the idea of starting something new. *I'll probably mess it up just as badly*, Lilou thought as they exited the bar. The air felt colder outside, and Lilou shivered. She looked at Marianne to see how her sister was adjusting to the frigid Pittsburgh air. Marianne zipped up the jacket and took Lilou by the hand.

"Come on, let's hurry back before I freeze here. I forgot all about the snow and the cold!" Marianne clutched at her jacket. They walked briskly side-by-side. There were few passersby, but they heard music and laughter coming from the bars.

Lilou looked left and right, taking in the night scene. The evening with her sister was the first time she visited Walnut Street after dark in years. *Why have I been limiting myself?* Lilou thought. With Marianne by her side, the world seemed open and friendly. Lilou felt exhilarated by her own bravery. The cold air felt refreshing. She wasn't tired, despite having spent all day in the office. And then she remembered.

"You know, I got promoted today," she told Marianne.

"At your company? That's fantastic! You know, you never told me what you do there," Marianne noted. "Boy, it's cold out!"

"We do audits," Lilou responded. "You know I do Maman's accounting, too?"

"No, I had no idea! It must be crazy having to deal with her. Did she make you?" Marianne giggled.

"No, I wanted to do it, and things kind of just happened," Lilou said. She had grown to be one with the profession and could not remember a time when she wasn't balancing columns and adding up numbers.

"You've always been a little genius!" Marianne smiled at her softly and Lilou shook her head. She turned to Marianne and gasped. Her body knew it was him before her brain registered his face. Lilou's knees buckled, and she leaned on Marianne. Beads of cold sweat appeared on her forehead. Gary was standing across the street. Speaking to someone else and was half-turned away from the sisters, but Lilou knew it was him.

"Come on, let's move faster," Lilou said, feeling faint.

"Are you alright?" Marianne asked, giving her a concerned look, but fastening her pace.

"Linda, Linda, wait!" Lilou heard a familiar voice calling after her.

"It's a cop," Marianne looked back and hissed, pulling Lilou by the sleeve. "Do you know him?"

"A cop?" Lilou stopped and turned around. Only then did she notice he was wearing a police uniform. He was out of breath and an uncertain smile crossed his face.

"Linda, hi!" He smiled and his eyes sparkled. Lilou felt as if she were on the verge of collapsing. Fear gripped her stomach, and she clenched her fists. "Long time, I, I wanted to talk to you, ask you out, you know." Gary gave a half-smile. Lilou swallowed hard, unable to respond.

"Hi, I am Marianne, Linda's sister." Marianne extended her hand.

"Her sister? You ran off a while back, didn't you?" Gary narrowed his eyes and examined Marianne.

Lilou stepped back, grateful to be forgotten for even a moment. *Maybe he will leave, and then things can return to normal.* Her heart beat so fast, she was sure it would jump out of her chest.

"How do you know that?" Marianne frowned. "I don't think we've met."

"I used to live across the street from your house, neighbors talk." Gary nodded at Marianne and then fixed his gaze on Lilou.

Why is he speaking like nothing happened? Does he not remember? Did he forgive me? Lilou thought. She surreptitiously examined Gary's face. Suddenly, her old feelings for him came flooding back. It was like being slammed with a wave of emotion so strong she could not control it. The very feelings that she'd been trying to suppress for several years burst out at once and overpowered her. Lilou was back to the time when she watched Gary, dreamed of him, thought of him, wanted to know his every movement and thought. She was back to the time when she had been certain that the two of them would be together. That she and Gary were destined for each other. It was as if all the obstacles that had separated the two of them washed away and she finally had the man she'd dreamed of. Lilou was certain that they would be together now.

"Gary," Lilou said his name softly.

"Hey, Linda, so I was just thinking, I'd wanted to come by, ask you out. What do you say?"

"Yes," Lilou nodded. "Sounds good." Things would work out perfectly this time, of that she was sure. A happy smile crossed her face.

"Alright, then, I'll come by. After Thanksgiving, I'll be off next Friday night, December 3rd. We can go watch a movie or something?

Lilou's entire world had turned around. It was him, her old Gary, the one who had never been with Sammy, who had never gotten married, who hadn't drunkenly made a move on her. They were meant to be together, the two of them, and soon that vision would become a reality.

"Yes, sounds good," Lilou said, only then realizing that she had just repeated herself.

"See you next Friday," Gary said.

"Nice meeting you, Gary." Marianne threw an assessing look at the man as they walked away. "Lilou, are you going to tell me what's going on? Are you guys seeing each other?" Marianne asked a few minutes later, when they turned the corner.

"No, he's just a neighbor. Well, a former neighbor, he lives in those buildings, over there." Lilou pointed at a distance and blushed, as the recollection of the events that took place in Gary's apartment flooded her thoughts.

"He seems to like you, that's for sure. So you never went out with him?" Marianne stopped and stared at Lilou who was forced to stop as well. Marianne looked at her with concern, and for a moment Lilou considered telling her sister the truth about what had happened. Then Lilou stopped herself.

Who knows what Marianne would think? Lilou thought. She remembered how she'd told Aline about Gary and how easy it was to lie about him. Then, for a brief moment, the memory of the spell, the candle, the blood and wine in a glass, flashed in her mind. In a habitual fashion, she pushed the memory away.

"We kind of did, but then things ended." A tear rolled down Lilou's face as she presented an alternative version of events.

"So why are you talking to him now? You still like him?" Marianne touched Lilou's arm.

"I guess so," Lilou shrugged as they reached their house.

"You should just give him a chance. Seems nice, and he is a cop, so you'll always feel protected." Marianne opened the front door and winked at her sister.

"Yeah," Lilou giggled in response

"Maman, Daddy, we are home!" Marianne yelled out.

"Come on in. We are in the kitchen!" The sisters heard their mother's voice. For a moment, Lilou felt as if Marianne had never left, and as if her life had always been like that. Normal.

Chapter 22
COURTSHIP

Thanksgiving at the Kellehers that year was a joyous experience. Marianne's return united the family. Even Katrine, normally full of nervous energy, was calmer. The sisters helped their mother with the cooking, and the three of them prepared the Thanksgiving turkey together. Katrine insisted, as usual, to stuff it with chestnuts, following a French recipe, and Marianne and Lilou helped to roast and peel the chestnuts, jokingly complaining of how long the process took. Marianne prepared a potato salad that she loved eating in California, and Katrine graciously admitted that it was delicious.

Their Thanksgiving dinner was festive. They said words of gratitude and listened to Marianne, who shared stories of her travails at the farm. They celebrated Lilou's success at work, and talked about the future, where they would be together again as a family.

Lilou did her best to enjoy the time with her family, but thoughts of Gary occupied her mind. Thanksgiving weekend passed, and Lilou returned to her regular routine of working twelve hours a day, and only then was she able to stop obsessing over Gary.

By the time the following Friday came, the prospect of going on a date with Gary no longer seemed real. Gary had not called, had not reconfirmed, and Lilou doubted she would be going out with him at all. Right after meeting Gary again, Lilou allowed herself to dream, but now, with the uncertainty of the date, fear was creeping in.

What if he cancels? What if he doesn't want me? Lilou thought, as she sat on her bed, staring at her feet. It was Friday and she had just gotten home from work. Lilou wiggled her toes and noticed that one of her toenails was long. She rose to get nail clippers.

That's when she saw a tiny hand sticking out from under the bed. It was smaller than a child's in size, but was shaped like an adult hand, with hairs on the knuckles. Lilou jumped on the bed, suppressing a scream. She peered under the bed. The tiny hand was not immediately visible, but Lilou saw a shape closer to the wall. She rose and grabbed the bed in order to move it when Marianne walked in.

"Lilou, hi, do you want to borrow the green…" Her sister stopped in the middle of a sentence. "What are you up to?"

"Nothing." Lilou lied.

"You need help? Did you drop something?"

"Yes, umm, nothing, was just moving the bed back," Lilou said.

"I was just thinking I could help you get ready," Marianne said, the look on her face earnest.

"Yes, thank you," Lilou nodded. She took Marianne's appearance in her room as a sign that the date would go on as planned. *I guess I should get ready,* a thought flashed through her mind and immediately fueled dreams of a happy future with Gary.

"You want to wear this one again? It looked good on you." Marianne produced the green halter top Lilou had borrowed from her.

"Yes, sounds great!" Lilou took it and held it against her chest. "I love the color," she tried to give her voice a perky tone.

"Lilou, don't worry, it'll be fine. The guy clearly likes you, just be yourself." Marianne gave her a reassuring smile. Lilou averted her eyes, too nervous to react.

At six in the evening, Lilou came downstairs, dressed for her date. Marianne was behind her. They had agreed that Marianne would let their parents know about Lilou's plans with Gary.

"Maman, Daddy, Lilou is going out," Marianne said. Lilou admired the casual tone of her sister's voice.

"Great. What time will the two of you be back?" Michael asked.

"It's just Lilou, she's going out," Marianne added.

"What? Why not the two of you together?" Katrine came out of the kitchen, drying her hands on a towel.

"She's going out with a friend."

"What friend is that?" Their father approached.

"It's Gary, he is taking me out on a date Daddy," Lilou responded, her cheeks turning red.

"Gary? Which Gary's that?" Michael Kelleher gave Lilou a confused look.

"You know, the one from across the street? He's a police officer now."

"A cop? That's not bad, when did he become a cop?" Michael nodded in approval. "That's a manly profession, not bad, not bad."

"Michael, he dropped out of college, remember, Dorothy told us, and then finished the police academy last year," her mother said.

"Gary, that Gary, of course, but didn't he get married? Linda, what's going on?"

"He got divorced," Lilou responded, and immediately a feeling of doom creeped in. *What if he is still with Sammy?* A knot formed in her stomach.

"Divorced? So what does he want with you? Isn't he the one who was at the party?"

"Daddy, it's not a big deal," she said, surprised that her father remembered. They had not discussed Gary's role in Lilou's fainting episode, and Lilou thought her father had not paid attention that Gary was next to her when she fainted.

"I don't understand. Where has this guy been for the last two years then?" Michael insisted.

"Michael, please just let it be. Lilou is an adult," Katrine said.

"I just don't want any surprises." Michael's face looked severe. "What time will you be back?"

Lilou was trying to come up with a reasonable answer when there was a knock at the door. The four Kellehers exchanged glances, and then, as if they had rehearsed the scene beforehand, Marianne pulled Lilou away from the door and into the living room. Katrine and Michael moved into the kitchen and then Marianne slowly approached the front door. She yelled out 'who is it?', her voice casual with a tone of surprise.

A few seconds later Lilou heard Gary's voice. "I am here for Linda."

Lilou turned red with pleasure. *My Gary is here! He is going to take me on a date! Our first official date!*

"Hi, Gary." Lilou appeared from the shadows. She

noticed that the green top she was wearing shimmered in the light. For a moment, Lilou imagined herself as a mermaid, beautiful, glittering, magical. Her eyes lit up, and Lilou moved to the light, so that Gary could see her face. She had applied rouge earlier to accentuate her cheekbones.

"Hey, Linda, are you ready?" Gary gave her a piercing look.

"I am!" Lilou shook her head with enthusiasm.

At that moment, her father walked up to them and extended his hand to Gary. "Nice to see you again, Gary. I hear you've joined the police force?"

"Yes, Mr. Kelleher, I graduated from the police academy last year." Gary's face lit up.

"Congratulations, great to hear that." Lilou's father cleared his throat. "Well, I won't keep you. Have fun."

He didn't tell us what time I should be back, Lilou noticed, and hurried after Gary outside.

"I just bought a car." Gary pointed to a black vehicle parked out front. "1971 Mustang Mach 1!" He checked Lilou's face for a reaction. She tried to express enthusiasm. "You like it? Paid top dollar! This baby is fast! And the motor roars!" Gary announced as he unlocked the car.

"Great!" Lilou smiled back, working hard to stay calm. She wanted to fast-forward to the part of their relationship when Gary professed his feelings for her, when they were a happy couple, living together in their house, together at last.

"So, I thought, we could see *Rocky.*" Gary opened the car door for her, and Lilou's heart leaped. *He's a gentleman!* she thought, giving him a gentle smile. "It's a movie about this guy in Philly, real awesome. He's a boxer, an under-dog." Gary gesticulated excitedly as they drove. "We'll go see it at the Manor," Gary added and fell silent. He looked over at Lilou. His silence jerked her out of her thoughts, and she forced herself to pay attention to what was happening. The last thing she heard was 'the Manor', and Lilou guessed that they would see a movie. She'd missed all that Gary had said about the film, and now struggled to give her face an engaged look.

"That's great," Lilou said, hoping that the vagueness of her words would be enough to give Gary the right impression. She struggled to pay attention to him and to what was happening around her. Her imagination was miles away, in the future, where the fantasy Gary and she were happy and in love.

"I am excited to watch it, you know," Gary added. "And with you, it's special." He coughed. The car revved up as they went up the steep hill of South Negley Avenue, inching up at an almost 45% angle. Lilou hated going up this street in the winter, worrying that it would be too icy, and imagined sliding back and hitting the car behind them. A part of her imagination also pictured the car defying the laws of gravity and flipping back, rolling down the street all the way to Fifth Avenue. But Gary did not share her worries, and so they went up the hill and were now crossing Wilkins. A few minutes later, they parked on Murray Avenue, right across from the Manor Theater. Gary did not open her door to let her out of the car. *But he opened the door to let me in. I guess it balances out,* Lilou decided as she followed Gary into the theater.

Lilou paid little attention to the movie. She had trouble concentrating on the plot, Sylvester Stallone and his nearly always mute face that popped in and out of the screen made little sense to her. When the sad, dedicated features of his love interest appeared, Lilou perked up. She imagined herself in place of the faithful Adrian and dreamed of being just like her, at the side of a champion. As the lights came on and the credits rolled, Lilou looked over at Gary and noticed tears in his eyes.

"This movie is going to be my favorite. I've gotta go see it again," he said. They made their way outside, and Gary took her by the hand. "Linda, I wanted to talk to you, you know." His voice cracked as he said this, and Lilou's hands felt like icicles. *He is going to bring it up,* she thought, *I can't talk to him about it.* Lilou froze in place. "There's this place, right down the street, let's talk over there."

Before she could react, Gary led Lilou to Silky's. The place was dimly lit and nearly empty. "Sit right here." Gary pointed to a table with two stools and disappeared. Lilou stared at her nails. Lilou remembered the manicure she'd gotten right before running into Gary that day over two years ago, and a shiver ran down her spine. She'd kept her nails short ever since.

"Here you go." Gary placed two beers on the table, and Lilou wondered if her outings to bars would always involve drinking beer.

She took a polite sip, noticing how the tips of her fingers got even colder upon touching the glass.

"Listen, Linda, I wanna tell you, I've been doing a lot of thinking." He pulled up a chair and sat across from her. Gary reached for her right hand and took it into his. "Your hand is so cold. Let me warm it up for you."

Lilou felt like she couldn't breathe. Her heart beat incredibly fast. *Is he going to apologize? What's happening?* Their table wobbled and some of the beer spilled. Before Gary could continue speaking, Lilou jumped off the stool.

"I'll go get a napkin, one second." She galloped to the bar, grateful for an excuse to leave. When she returned a moment later, Gary had a sad expression on his face. Lilou tapped the spilled beer and was about to leave when Gary intercepted her.

"Please, have a seat, Linda," he pleaded.

"Sure, but the beer, it's going to smell," Lilou offered an explanation, clutching the wet napkin in her hands.

"It doesn't matter. I need to tell you. You know, when we met, that time." Gary averted his eyes. "I am sorry about what happened. It was a real low point for me. I am sorry if I upset you." Lilou suppressed a cry. She swallowed hard, unable to react. Gary's apology did not align with her dream of their future together. She would love him no matter what, apology or not. She needed to convey that to Gary somehow. Lilou turned to face Gary.

"I understand. It's not a big deal," she said.

"It's not?"

"No, not at all." Lilou forced a smile. It came out crooked.

"I just thought I really messed up. I was drinking so much back then. Sammy'd just left me. We had some issues. Sammy would fist-fight me, punch me. It was crazy." Gary sighed.

"She left you?" Lilou stared at Gary. A knot formed in her stomach. The image of Gary and Sammy, their wedding, the miniature bride standing fiercely by Gary's side, guarding her territory from Lilou.

"Yeah, decided I was no good," Gary shrugged. "I guess I wasn't a good husband. I wasn't ready back then to get married."

"I understand." Lilou nodded. She agreed with the fact that Gary's wedding had been a mistake. And not just because it was in a rush. *Gary should have married me*, Lilou thought.

"I should have married you, Linda." She stared at Gary in stunned silence. Lilou's fantasy world and reality collided.

"Married me?" Lilou repeated, looking carefully at Gary.

"Yes, I should have married you, Linda. You are the perfect girl for me. I am okay now, I will be a good husband." Gary was speaking fast. He grabbed her hands and held them tightly in his. Lilou noticed that his cheek twitched slightly. "After that year, and everything, I cleaned up real good, went to the police academy, and now, I've been a police officer for almost a year, it's a good job, stable. And I don't run around no more."

"Yes," Lilou agreed.

"Linda, after that time, I couldn't stop thinking about you. I kept thinking about you, but that party, all that. I wanted to come and see you, but I didn't want you to turn me away."

Lilou fidgeted, hearing Gary's words. *Is this real? Am I dreaming?*

"I need a good woman by my side, and I'll never find better than you, Linda." Gary concluded and gave her an expectant look.

"Oh," Lilou nodded.

"Are you saying yes?"

"I am!" Lilou nodded. Happy tears filled her eyes. She was engaged! Gary had just asked her to marry him and she said yes. She had a fiancé, a future husband. Soon, her life would be complete with a family of her own. She could tell her colleagues at work that she was engaged. Lilou pictured amazement on the faces of Mr. Bradford and Larry Coleman. She would soon marry a police officer! Strong and smart. *I was right all along. We were destined to be together!* Lilou smiled at the thought.

"Oh, Linda! I am so glad!" Gary said. "I'll buy you an engagement ring for Christmas. What do you think?"

"That's perfect! I guess Christmas is right around the corner!" She smiled.

"When should we tell your parents? I gotta talk to your dad, right?" A look of worry crossed Gary's face.

"Maybe next weekend?" Lilou shrugged. What did her parents' reaction matter now that she would have a husband? Gary would marry her!

Her dream was coming true and nothing else mattered.

Chapter 23
THE WEDDING

When setting the date of her wedding, Lilou checked with her sister to make sure it would work for her and the farm.

"Lilou, please don't worry about me," Marianne had told her on the phone.

"No, Marianne, I need you at the wedding and I don't want to make things more difficult for you," Lilou responded.

"I will come to your wedding no matter what!" Marianne yelled into the receiver, but Lilou could tell that her sister appreciated being asked. "The only thing would be Frank. Both of us wouldn't be able to leave the farm. So he won't be able to be there, that's all."

"That's okay, Marianne, I hope to meet him some other time," Lilou responded with a sigh.

"Of course, you guys should come out for your honeymoon!" Marianne offered.

"That would be lovely! I just have to figure out my leave plans," Lilou responded and frowned, glad that Marianne could not see her face. She had been agonizing over the honeymoon for several weeks now. She and Gary had planned the wedding in early May so that it would be after the April 15th tax deadlines, but being so busy right before the wedding meant that Lilou had not had time to plan a honeymoon. Gary left all the preparations to her, and Lilou spent most of her free time discussing wedding arrangements with her parents and going over guest lists and RSVPs. The time right before April 15th she worked twelve-hour days in the office, and then came home with so much work that she would collapse on her bed, exhausted.

"Linda, this isn't healthy." Her father hovered over her, concern on his face, when Lilou was sitting in the kitchen one evening, eating her dinner, while staring at an open file with spreadsheets.

"What isn't healthy?" Lilou asked, chewing.

"This, you are so busy! You are about to get married, change your life. You need to get into the right state of mind before the wedding." Her father sat down next to her.

"Daddy, please, I am fine," Lilou responded, flipping through the folder, but her mind was no longer on her work. Worry crept in. *What if Daddy is right?* she wondered.

"Listen, sweetheart, I am speaking from experience. Marriage is going to change your life. You shouldn't rush into it. Consider postponing the wedding."

"Daddy, but Gary would be upset with me. He might think I am having doubts."

"Linda, if that's the case, you shouldn't marry him in the first place. He needs to understand how much your work means to you. He isn't blind, is he? He can see how overworked you are!"

"It's fine, Daddy, I am used to it," Lilou responded and took another bite of the pasta her mother had prepared. She could barely taste what she was eating.

"I am telling you, marriage will mean new responsibilities. Make sure you are ready!" Her father said and rose from his seat.

Lilou was not about to postpone anything. *How hard can marriage be?* she thought, finishing her dinner. *I am finally going to be with my first love!* Lilou couldn't wait to get married, grateful to finally be with Gary. Her dream was about to come true, they would be together, a happy couple with only love and joy on the horizon. Lilou imagined how Gary would return home from work, she would greet him with a freshly cooked meal, and they would snuggle in front of a TV, watching a show together. *I guess a honeymoon isn't that important.* Lilou shrugged, as she rose to put her plate in the sink.

Her mother got her wedding dress from one of her clients, who worked at Kaufmann's department store.

"Lilou, this was a great deal, and look how pretty it is." Katrine produced the gown, long with a flowing skirt and lace-covered sleeves.

"Thank you, Maman." Lilou held the dress against her waist.

"I made sure the sleeves were long, told Pamela, too," Katrine noted.

"Thank you, Maman." Remembering Sammy's tiny biceps that were prominently displayed at Gary's wedding, Lilou had instructed her mother to find her a dress that was completely different from Samantha's. Her own dress was long, flowing, and the sleeves covered her arms. It fit her well, and Lilou took it as a sign that stars had aligned in her favor. The universe itself was supporting her wedding to Gary.

After proposing to her on December 3rd, Gary told her they shouldn't sleep together and stay chaste until marriage. "I've changed, Linda. I want us to start our marriage on the right note." His face was solemn as he said those words, and Lilou immediately agreed.

In the short time right before the wedding, Gary and Lilou saw each other just once a week. It wasn't easy because of Gary's shifts that almost always fell on weekends, and Lilou's demanding work schedule during the work week. Lilou wondered how he had managed to take her to see *Rocky* on a Friday night. *That date night was a miracle,* Lilou thought fondly of the evening when her world changed. *December 3rd is going to be my favorite day for the rest of my life,* Lilou decided. The day of Gary's proposal was etched prominently in her mind. She added and subtracted numbers and consulted numerology books to understand whether the day was fortuitous. The numbers of December 3rd, 1976 added up to 29.

29 is great, Lilou thought, and remembered her math books. *It's produced by three consecutive squares.* But the number's mathematical originality did not provide a response to its mystical significance. According to one numerology book, it needed to be reduced further, and adding 2 and 9 produced 11.

11 is definitely magical, it's two ones together, it's like they are next to each other, beautiful and aligned, just like Gary and me. Lilou began doodling the number everywhere, on her paperwork, notebooks, even her hand.

Her fascination with the number came to an abrupt stop several days before the wedding, when she went to an occult shop on Walnut Street. She'd stumbled upon it one day, and had since visited it a few times, despite being extremely busy. This time she walked in, and the first thing she saw were two long candles standing side by side.

Just like the number 11, our number, Lilou thought, but then she remembered Aline and the spell. The memory of what had happened in Lyon had been pushed so far back that retrieving it caused Lilou great pain. It was like a jolt of electricity. She was suddenly carried back to her cousin's bedroom, seeing everything so vividly that she even felt the cut of the razor blade on the tip of her index finger, as Aline drew her blood. Lilou turned pale. "A witch! I am going to be a witch!" She remembered Aline saying the words.

That spell, Gary, what I did. It was nothing, Lilou thought. Her stomach was in knots and she had to crouch in the corner of the shop to avoid fainting. *I should have told Grand-mère about the spell.*

"Are you alright?" The shop assistant asked. It was always the same girl, who called herself Sunflower. Lilou had gotten to know the girl with raven black hair, and wondered why she'd picked that name for herself. Lilou suspected Sunflower lived in the shop.

"I, yes, I am fine," Lilou responded, gasping for air. *What Aline and I did was nothing, it was just some silly stuff.* Lilou calmed herself and got up. Black circles floated in front of her eyes as she headed for the exit.

"You take care, Linda," Sunflower called after her.

THE DAY of the wedding came. Lilou stared at her wedding dress hanging on the closet door. She was twisting the narrow band of her engagement ring on her finger. The diamond was small, the band itself tiny, but that didn't matter. Lilou had an engagement ring with an actual diamond in it! Her mind flashed back to the proposal, and she felt tears of joy in her eyes. That romantic night when they went to see *Rocky*, Gary's earnest face, his apology. *He said that he should have married me!* Lilou went back to her favorite part of the memory.

"Lilou!" she heard her mother's voice. There was the sound of heels clanking on the steps and a moment later, her mother appeared, holding a box with Mary Kay cosmetics in her hands. "I am thinking these colors, not too muted, nice festive tones," Katrine chirped.

"Thank you, Maman," Lilou said.

"I don't know why you refuse to have your hair done. You could go back to that salon."

"It's fine, Maman, I will just pull it back, and Marianne can help me set it," Lilou tensed. She hadn't been to the Shadyside salon in almost three years and was not about to go back. She considered the place to be bad luck.

"Fine, but it just makes things harder. You want to look your best, don't you? Anyway, I invited Lesley over. She'll help with your hair."

"Who's Lesley?" Marianne walked in, holding hair pins and a brush.

"One of my clients, she's very good at styling, almost a professional. I mean, of course, going to a professional would be the sensible thing to do, but at least it's something."

"So you don't need me to do anything?" Marianne let out a breath.

"Please stay, Marianne," Lilou reached for her sister's hand and smiled at her sister. Marianne made everything better. Lilou thought back to their night out, when the two of them had run into Gary together. Marianne's presence was like a lucky charm. *If it weren't for Marianne and her return, I wouldn't be marrying Gary,* Lilou thought.

It took two hours to get Lilou's hair done, and the process left her exhausted. Now she was preparing to put on the dress without destroying her hair. She moved her hand to feel the hairdo, but her mother yelled out a warning: "No, Lilou, you'll ruin it!" And Lilou jerked her hand back.

"We should have had her wear the dress all along!" Katrine sighed, turning to Marianne.

"But the corset!" Marianne protested. "Here, Lilou, let me hold it for you." Her sister opened the dress, and Lilou carefully put it on.

"How beautiful she looks!" Katrine clapped her hands.

"She does!" Marianne nodded and gave her sister an approving look. Lilou's heart leaped. With her sister and mother at her side, she felt loved. Marianne fixed Lilou's hair that had come undone, while Katrine did Lilou's make-up.

▭

THE WEDDING CEREMONY took place at the Presbyterian church in Shadyside, and the reception was in the Kellehers' back yard. It took Lilou some time to convince her parents to host the event. They thought that the garden wedding might remind people of Lilou's fainting episode at her graduation party. Lilou insisted on having the reception at her parents' backyard because her childhood home was a place that was safe from Sammy's influence. It was her own territory.

Throughout the ceremony, Lilou felt on edge. First she was afraid that Gary would be late, then she was anxious that her feet would start hurting standing so long in heels. Then she worried she would start sweating through the dress, or that the veil would come undone, or that her hair would unravel. Or that she would get a headache from the hairspray that had been so abundantly sprayed on her head that her hair felt stiff and could almost stand on its own.

Lilou paid little attention to the words of the priest, with whom she and Gary had met separately, and who had agreed to officiate their wedding. When the ceremony finished without incident, Lilou was genuinely surprised. She and Gary kissed, and the guests clapped. Lilou stared in awe at her ring finger, with two narrow bands now adorning it.

"Let me see," he asked, and Lilou extended her hand to him. Gary kissed it and then pulled her towards him. "I love you," he murmured into Lilou's ear. "I can't wait until tonight."

"I love you, too," Lilou purred back, and then added silently to herself *more than you'll ever know.*

At the reception, Lilou's anxiety dissipated and she enjoyed the party. A huge sign reading 'Congratulations, Gary and Linda!' adorned the backyard. Lilou stared at the sign. She counted the number of letters in their names. It was nine, no matter which version of her name she used, and Lilou thought it a good sign. She then thought about her new last name. Blacklin. *Eight letters. Mrs. Blacklin. Mrs. Gary Blacklin.* A radiant smile crossed her face.

In a few hours, Lilou would enter her new home. She did not expect everything to happen so quickly, but Gary's lease was ending, and she saw a beautiful home for sale in their neighborhood, near her parents' home, on South Highland Avenue. Lilou never doubted that she would want to stay in Shadyside and Gary agreed. Lilou's parents helped with the down payment, and she also added from her savings. After nearly three years at Pedersen Accountants, Lilou had saved a considerable sum.

Although it crossed her mind to ask Gary to contribute, she decided against it. *He only started his job a year ago;* she thought fondly. *He works so hard. And he spent money on the ring.*

Lilou fiddled with the narrow band on her ring finger.

Lilou's name was the only one on the title and the mortgage because the purchase was made before she and Gary got married. At the closing, Lilou wrote the first check, and felt a tear in her eye as she became a proud homeowner.

"You are one of the first women to get a mortgage with us," the banker told her in confidence, after Lilou signed all the documents. "Congratulations on your upcoming nuptials. Once you get married, come back. We'll update the documents for you." He adjusted his glasses.

"Update the documents?" Lilou gave him a quizzical look. She'd been so focused on getting everything ready for the wedding, and now, with the home purchase, she badly wanted to get the home ready for her wedding night.

"Yes, you'll want to add your husband to the title and the mortgage," the banker stated in a tone that did not accommodate contradictions.

"Of course," Lilou nodded, took the folder with the documents, and promptly forgot about the conversation.

It was thanks to Katrine that the home was ready for the newlyweds. Lilou's mother had located a handyman and got the kitchen and the bedroom ready for the wedding night.

"Lilou, this is the best I can do," Katrine said.

"Thank you, Maman!" Lilou responded. Changes in her life were happening so fast that she could barely keep track. A new chapter was about to begin.

At midnight, as the party ended, Gary looked at her. He held up a glass of champagne. "To my wife!" he said and kissed Lilou on the lips.

Her face turned bright red, and her eyes glistened with pleasure. Gary took her by the hand and led her to his Mustang.

"Gary, should you be driving?" Lilou asked.

"I am fine! It's just a few blocks. Get in, wife!" he said and chuckled.

She obliged, and they drove the three blocks to their new home. Once there, Lilou fumbled for the keys, with Gary leaning on her. She could feel his drunken breath, and it made her feel nauseous.

Lilou pushed the feeling away.

"Hurry up," Gary urged, as she unlocked the door. "I gotta go real bad," he said and rushed to the bathroom.

Lilou entered her new home and stood by the door. She had expected Gary to carry her over the threshold, like she'd seen in the movies. *I wonder if it's bad luck that we came here like this.* She scanned the space. It was dark, and she was about to flip the switch on when she saw a pair of eyes staring back at her.

The same eyes she'd seen in her bedroom in her parents' home. Lilou let out a scream. She lunged forward and flicked on the light. Lilou looked to check for the eyes.

There was nothing.

THE END

THANK YOU FOR READING 'LILOU'. *If you enjoyed it, I would love your honest review on Amazon. Why am I asking for reviews? For an indie author like myself, each review means I can get more books to other readers who enjoy stories written in the magical realism style. This is why every single review means a huge amount to me.*

Thank you for your support. And above all, happy reading.

Lilou: Twenty-Seven
Generations of Magic
AN EXCERPT

Independence Day

July 4th, 1995

"Linda, Linda, move! You fell asleep in front of the TV again."

Lilou shivered, feeling her husband's hand on her shoulder, shaking her awake. The throw blanket shifted, and Lilou reached for it to cover herself. She badly wanted to finish her dream and figure out what happened next. She moaned, showing her protest, and closed her eyes.

"Linda, I gotta go to work, get up." Gary shook her leg. She twitched, trying to stay asleep, but the shake did its job. Lilou was now awake. She opened her eyes and sat up on the couch, immediately yelping in pain. Her neck felt sore – the result of spending the night curled up in an armchair.

"Oh Gary, why didn't you wake me up sooner?" Lilou sighed. "This armchair is terrible for my back." She stretched, carefully moving her shoulders back and forth, then craning her neck, trying to get the soreness out.

"That's old age, Linda. You are no spring chicken." He

gave her an appraising look. "And besides, last night I went out like a rock," Gary responded. He was fully dressed in uniform, and Lilou tensed.

"Honey, I thought you were off today?" Lilou tried to make her voice sound neutral, obsequious even, so as not to alert her husband to how anxious she felt.

"I'm on call, kitty cat." Gary frowned, the way he always did when he felt his wife was restricting his freedom of action.

"My parents are having a cookout, honey, July 4th, remember? They are expecting us." Lilou's voice cracked. She knew she was on the verge of making her husband snap. It took them months to make-up after Christmas and Gary didn't start speaking to her until mid-April. She definitely could not risk upsetting him again.

"I'll be there as soon as I'm free." Gary pursed his lips and gave Lilou a steely look. "Gotta go." He turned on his heels and was about to leave, when Lilou called after him:

"But my dad got that new grill, Gary, you guys talked about –"

"Linda, stop it, I gotta go," Gary interrupted her and opened the door.

Lilou knew she had been defeated. It was impossible to argue with her husband when he was in one of his moods. The memory of Gary's recent and longest silent treatment, which lasted until Easter, still fresh on her mind, Lilou said nothing else. More than anything, Lilou wanted the July 4th holiday to go well. Their two boys had just left for California and Lilou pictured an idyllic month of spousal bliss in her husband's company, as well as some badly needed rest.

The school year left Lilou feeling exhausted. Both of their boys were in high school, and she had to push her older son to take his schoolwork seriously and prepare for college, while managing her younger son's endless after-school activities. This was all on top of her job at Pedersen Accountants. After over twenty years there, she still hadn't made partner, and the situation was becoming increasingly more stressful. Lilou could not remember the last time she had a minute to herself.

"Gary, I gotta tell you something," Lilou called after her husband. She knew Gary would retaliate later, but wanted to hold him back, even for a moment longer. She followed him into the hallway.

"Now what?" He groaned, standing half-way through the door.

"Honey, I'm kind of embarrassed to tell you," Lilou hesitated, but she was already at a point of no return. "You know, honey, I had one of my dreams again."

"Another one? With the wolf?" Gary asked, squinting predatorily.

Lilou knew he was preparing to make a joke at her expense. From time to time, Lilou had strange dreams. Gary was aware of them, because sometimes she would say things in her sleep. She dreamt of strange creatures, a forest, and a wolf who was her protector. Gary was aware of a wolf, though not the fact that his name was Wolfgang.

For a moment she hesitated, but the dream had been so clear and had shaken her to her core. And Lilou made up her mind.

"Not the wolf. You see, honey, I dreamed that I wanted to poison you. With mushrooms. Death caps."

"Poison me? Death caps?" Gary rolled his eyes. "Why would you want to do that?"

The front door slammed shut and, a few seconds later, Lilou heard the sound of Gary's Ford starting.

Lilou: Twenty-Seven Generations of Magic

Scan to read Lilou: Twenty-Seven Generations of Magic. Book 2 in the Shadyside Chronicles Series

Exclusive Free Book

YOUR FREE BOOK IS WAITING...

Download your exclusive free copy of 'Katrine' and learn about the witchy upbringing of Lilou's mother.

Connect with the author

Website: www.sashkina.com

Email: sasha@sashkina.com

Thank you for reading 'Lilou'. If you enjoyed it, I would love your honest review on Amazon. Why am I asking for reviews? For an indie author like myself, each review means I can get more books to other readers who enjoy stories written in the magical realism style. This is why every single review means a huge amount to me.

Thank you for your support. And above all, happy reading.

About the Author

Alexandra Pugachevsky has always believed that magical elements exist in all aspects of our lives and reality is multi-dimensional. She writes in the magical realism genre.

Having immigrated to the United States from Moscow in her teens, Alexandra fell in love with the city of Pittsburgh, and has retained that love until now. She can't help but write about Pittsburgh. Another city she loves is Paris, which also features prominently in her work.

Alexandra has made the Washington, DC Metropolitan area her home for the last 25 years.

Notes

Chapter 4

1. Fr. a *term of endearment. Literately meaning 'my little cabbage' or 'my darling'*

Chapter 8

1. Sorry, dear (fr)

Chapter 9

1. exactly (fr)

Chapter 10

1. welcome to Lyon (fr)
2. In the car, Simone (fr)
3. Yes, Maman

Chapter 11

1. of course, of course
2. Unbelievable (fr)

Chapter 16

1. Like cures like (latin)

Chapter 20

1. Unbelievable (fr)

Acknowledgments

I am grateful to the Steel City for being my first home in the United States and for welcoming me with open arms. Pittsburgh continues to be a source of inspiration for me to this day, and I could not imagine a better setting for my books.

This book is dedicated to all the misfits, real and imaginary. May we all find a place where we belong.

www.ingramcontent.com/pod-product-compliance
Lightning Source LLC
Chambersburg PA
CBHW070504300726
48975CB00007B/2311